PRE-FIX

"Excuse me," someone said from behind her. "Can I ask you a question?"

Allie turned around to find their original waiter peering down at her. He was even better-looking close-up. She couldn't help but smile at him. "You just did, but go ahead and ask me another."

He handed Allie a scrap of paper. "Can you give your sister my number? I'd love to take her out sometime."

Allie kept her smile frozen on her face and took the scrap. "Sure," she said.

This type of thing had happened before, so she wasn't surprised.

What shocked her was the thought that popped into her head as she watched him walk away: If the waiter had seen Allie postsurgery, might he have given his number to her, instead?

Other timely reads from Simon Pulse

Crank by Ellen Hopkins

21 by Jeremy Iversen

Uglies trilogy by Scott Westerfeld

Massive by Julia Bell

Rx by Tracy Lynn

By Leslie Margolis

SIMON PULSE
NEW YORK · LONDON · TORONTO · SYDNEY

SIMON PULSE
An imprint of Simon & Schuster Children's Publishing Division
1230 Avenue of the Americas, New York, NY 10020

Designed by Steve Kennedy
The text of this book was set in ITC Charter
Manufactured in the United States of America
First Simon Pulse edition October 2006
10 9 8 7 6 5 4 3 2 1
Library of Congress Control Number 2005937170
ISBN-13: 978-1-4169-2456-2
ISBN-10: 1-4169-2456-6

ACKNOWLEDGMENTS

Many thanks to Bethany Buck, Emily Follas, Laura Langlie, Dr. Gerald H. Pitman, Kacey Long, Jim McGough, Fran Tiger, Ethan Wolff, Amanda McCormick, Jessica Ziegler, Mitchell Goldman, Judy Goldman, and Jim Margolis.

PROLOGUE

Cameron Beekman will never forget the day she learned that she was beautiful. It happened on a Monday, her first day of tenth grade and her first day, period, at Bel Air Prep Academy. She could even remember the exact time, 10:57, and her location, the second-floor girls' bathroom. To say that her life was never the same after that moment sounds insane, delusional, or at the very least like the beginning of a fairy tale, but it also happens to be the truth.

Before Dr. Glass fixed it, Cameron's nose was long and hooked, so that even when she was staring straight ahead, her nose pointed to the left. At her old school, they'd called her Beakface. Students wondered aloud how she defied gravity every day, keeping her head up when her big nose just had to be so heavy. They complained, *It's Beakface's fault that I'm failing. She sits in front of me, so I can't see the board.*

Sure, other kids had big noses too, but only Cameron's had

been singled out. And once she'd been labeled ugly, there was no going back. Or so she'd thought. As luck would have it, two weeks after her surgery, Cameron's family moved from La Jolla to Bel Air. All she'd ever wanted was to fade into the background, to be ignored rather than ridiculed, and now that she was transferring schools in September, she'd finally have that chance.

Imagine the scene: Cameron with her new nose, wandering through the halls at a different school, in her regulation navy blue blazer, starched white shirt, and itchy gray skirt. Yes, her uniform was horribly unstylish, but it was also just like everyone else's. She was blissfully anonymous and had never felt so free.

It wasn't until third-period Spanish class that everything started breaking down. Cameron sat at the back of the room, but for some reason two guys up front kept glancing back at her. They were cute, and that made her nervous. Cameron tried to ignore them. She focused on the blackboard, where her teacher, Señora Pesarro, was outlining students' responsibilities for the year: homework every night, an oral presentation each quarter, a term paper on Latin American history or literature . . .

Soon the stares escalated to whispers.

More students were in on it too. A girl with perfect, long, dark, curly hair and beautiful green eyes glanced over her shoulder at Cameron and giggled. Then she leaned over and whispered to the girl next to her. This one had straight red hair that stopped midway down her back. She wore blue and pink PUMAS rather than the school-sanctioned dark loafers.

Cameron could only think the worst—that the girls already hated her. But how had it happened so quickly? As memories from La Jolla flooded back, Cameron bit down on the insides of her cheeks and willed herself not to cry.

As soon as class ended, she ducked into the girls' bathroom. Since it was empty, she was able to stare at herself in the mirror and assess. Her new haircut framed her face in freshly dyed, blond, shoulder-length wisps. She'd shed her braces weeks before, and there was nothing caught in her teeth, which were now straight and gleaming white. She had a decent tan, and with her new nose, her big blue eyes were even more striking. As far as she could tell, she was completely normal-looking, so why the laughter?

Cameron wondered . . . Was there something in her posture that said, *I'm ugly*, or at least, *I* was *ugly?* La Jolla was one hundred and twenty-five miles from Bel Air, but had word traveled? Would she have to transfer again? Would her parents consider sending her to boarding school? Because maybe she'd have better luck out of state . . .

Suddenly the door flew open and in walked the dark-haired girl from Spanish class. Cameron pretended to be busy. Digging around in her backpack, she pulled out a lipstick and popped off the cap.

The girl watched as Cameron smoothed the color over her lips. Something about her—maybe it was the way she narrowed her eyes or perhaps it was her catlike stance—reminded Cameron of one of those lions from a show on the Discovery Channel, right before they attack their prey.

When they made eye contact, Cameron stood tall and braced herself for the inevitable put-down. She even came up with a couple of choice lines on her own, as if thinking them first herself would dilute the pain: *Are you trying to use your lips to distract us from your nose? It's so cute when ugly girls still try so hard.*

"I'm Lucy Mathers," the girl said instead, offering a perfectly manicured hand. Her nails were a deep, dark pink and just long enough to be elegant rather than tacky. "You're new?"

Cameron nodded. "Cameron Beekman." As they shook hands, Cameron expected Lucy to laugh and make the Beakface connection.

Instead, Lucy smiled warmly. "I love that shade. What's it called?"

Cameron flipped over the tube and read the bottom. "Um, 'Vixen.' Want to try?"

Without hesitation Lucy took the lipstick and turned to the mirror. "I got in trouble for this so many times last year, but it's not like anyone is going to give me detention on the first day."

"In trouble for what?" Cameron wondered.

Lucy laughed. "Wearing makeup," she said. "So rebellious. I like it."

Actually, Cameron had forgotten about Bel Air Prep's no-makeup rule, but she wasn't going to say so.

"You were in my Spanish class just now." It was a statement, not a question. Girls like Lucy didn't hedge. They didn't need to. "I should warn you about something. Know those two guys who kept looking at you?"

"Honestly? I hadn't noticed," Cameron lied, running her fingers through her bangs.

"Trust me, they were," said Lucy. "Tanner and Sanjay are their names, and they just flipped a coin to see who gets to ask you out first." Lucy rolled her pretty green eyes. "But I'd say forget them both. Sanjay is a total player and Tanner skipped a grade, so he's only fourteen. You'll probably want to date an upperclassman, anyway. Or at least someone with a car."

Too stunned to answer, all Cameron could do was blink. This girl was talking to her like she was normal. And not even just normal, but cool, like she was one of those girls who giggled over inside jokes with her friends, exchanged notes in the hall between classes, and talked about last Saturday's raging party. *Date an upperclassman,* she'd suggested. Cameron had never dated anyone.

Lucy must have mistaken her silence for indifference, because she went on talking. Moving from one subject to another, she reminded Cameron of a slick silver stone, expertly flung so that it skipped along the surface of the ocean. "The guys at our school aren't even that hot, I know. It's pretty lame. I keep asking my parents if I can transfer, but they're like, no way. It sucks. I can't stand it. Do you know that this school has stricter gym requirements than any other school in LA? And have you seen the uniforms they make us wear? Well, of course you have. You're wearing one. But did you check the tag on the blazer? It's a cotton-polyester blend, but they don't even tell you how much of it is polyester. It could be like 99.9 percent, which is so nasty. You know? It seriously gives me a rash. So who else do you have?"

No one so beautiful had ever talked to Cameron for this long without insulting her. She needed a few moments to process it all. Once she did, she pulled her schedule from her notebook and handed it over to Lucy, still not convinced that this wasn't an elaborate setup for some horribly cruel joke.

As Lucy surveyed it, her narrow eyebrows arched into perfect inverted V's. "Cool, we're in the same history class. English, too—that sucks for both of us. Mr. Turner gives a ton of homework and he wears the same brown jeans every single day."

Lucy handed back the schedule and linked her arm through Cameron's. "Come on, or we're gonna be late. I'm going right by your math class on my way to bio."

Still not quite believing what was happening, Cameron almost tripped as Lucy pulled her outside.

The next moments seemed to pass in slow motion. Before the door swung shut, Cameron looked over her shoulder for one last glance in the mirror. She hardly recognized the face that stared back at her.

The 10:57 late bell chimed, but to Cameron it sounded more like a game-winning buzzer. Fitting, because as far as she was concerned, she was walking away with the grand prize: Suddenly, almost magically, Cameron had been labeled as, and had therefore transformed into, one of the beautiful people.

CHAPTER ONE

SUMMER, ALMOST THREE YEARS LATER . . .

The plot was a familiar one. Cameron had seen it in plenty of movies, on TV, and in books. The nerdy girl ingratiates herself with the in crowd—by way of a makeover, or through dating a popular guy, or via some magical spell—only to find that the crowd she's been coveting is not very desirable at all. The girls are shallow, cruel, insensitive, and even dull. And the guys? Complete boneheads. But all of those stories got it wrong. Being beautiful translated into being popular, and being popular was even better than winning the lottery. Money couldn't buy happiness, and eventually it ran out. Being watched, envied, and desired? It never got old. Popularity was the ultimate high.

Sometimes Cameron had a hard time believing just how far she'd come. Yet here she was, eighteen years old and a high school graduate, on vacation in Cabo San Lucas, Mexico, for five whole days.

Stepping out onto the second-story balcony of the beach house, Cameron breathed in the clean, sea-salt-tinged air and looked around. The house was perched on a hill in between the mountains and the Sea of Cortez and surrounded by a garden of cacti, palm trees, and bright pink bougainvillea. The sun radiated through a cloudless sky, warming the air to a perfect eighty-five degrees. Cameron could hear the gentle, rhythmic crashing of waves from every room in the house.

Her four best friends were splayed out on lounge chairs poolside, like dolls living in Barbie's Dream House. Cameron aimed her camera down at them and began shooting. The scene was idyllic: utopia on an ocean-lined desert. Sure, there were also ten identical houses on either side of them, but if you knew how to capture it at the correct angle—and Cameron did—it would look like a magnificent oasis.

She took a picture of Lucy first, which made sense. It was Lucy who had the vacation house, and it was Lucy who'd convinced her parents that the girls were fully capable of taking a vacation on their own. (They'd all been to the Cabo house before, but never unchaperoned.)

Cameron aimed carefully, framing her friend in the center of the shot, and also including small wedges of sky, sea, bleached concrete, and pool.

Lucy had a swimmer's body, lean and muscular, and a swimmer's tan, which looked even more dramatic in contrast to her turquoise bikini. Her long curls draped over one shoulder, and her green eyes were hidden behind dark, oversized sunglasses. Cameron guessed she was sleeping, because otherwise the scene wouldn't be nearly as peaceful.

Moving her camera to the left, Cameron shot Ashlin, who was very much awake. She sat in the shade of a white umbrella to protect her pale, "twenty minutes in the sun and I'll fry like bacon" skin. Ashlin's sunglasses sat propped on her head, holding back her shoulder-length red hair, presumably so she'd have a clearer view of the *Us Weekly* in her lap. Next to her was a stack of equally trashy magazines, *People*, *Entertainment Weekly*, and *Star* included.

Even though she'd graduated as the school's valedictorian and was on her way to Stanford, Ashlin obsessed over celebrity culture. Who was cheating with whom and on what movie set? Which actor attacked a photographer on the streets of New York? What band trashed a hotel suite in Vegas? Ashlin actually cared. She devoured the tabloid magazines as if they were rows of chocolate cupcakes and she'd been dieting for months. She was the only person Cameron knew who could make allusions to Kafka's magical realism one second and the latest episode of *The OC* the next.

Cameron moved her camera to the other side of the clear, blue swimming pool to shoot Taylor and Hadley together.

This also made perfect sense, since the two were inseparable. They looked, sounded, and acted so similar that even their teachers got them confused.

They were both blond, but only Hadley was naturally so, and they both had green eyes, although Taylor's were green because of color contacts. Now their twin-pigtailed heads were huddled over a cell phone as they text-messaged someone.

Before Cameron had finished shooting them, though, Hadley put down the phone, yawned, and turned over onto her stomach.

Unsurprisingly, Taylor did the same just a few moments later.

Cameron lowered her camera. Sometimes it annoyed her, the way Taylor always followed Hadley around, looking to Hadley for answers. In the back of her mind, Cameron knew it bothered her so much because she feared she and Lucy shared a similar dynamic. But she couldn't help that. If Lucy hadn't talked to her three years ago, on that fateful first day of tenth grade, she wouldn't be where she was now. She might not have ever realized she was beautiful, or that she could be more than a quiet, studious girl who clutched her books too close to her chest and did her best to stay out of everyone's way. She might have ended up like Grace, her one friend from La Jolla, who dressed all in black, wore too much dark eyeliner, and sat silently in the back of class, obsessively reading Kurt Vonnegut. So of course she was eternally grateful.

"Pervert on the balcony!" Lucy yelled, suddenly awake.

Everyone looked up, and as they saw Cameron with her camera, a flurry of activity ensued. Ashlin spread her magazine over her hips. Hadley and Taylor both screamed and rolled over, wrapping their towels around their bodies.

"Put the camera down. Now!" Taylor yelled, crossing her fingers as if to ward off the devil.

The way they reacted, one would have thought Cameron was pointing some sort of assault rifle, rather than her new digital camera (a Canon single-lens reflex, the best graduation gift ever), at them.

Only Lucy surveyed the scene coolly. Propping herself up on her elbows and tilting her head to one side, she called, "I get veto power. Come down here and show us what you've got."

"Hold on," Cameron replied, before doing just that. Once she and more importantly her camera were down by the pool, everyone huddled around.

Ashlin turned it on and started going through the pictures displayed on the digital screen in back. "Oh my gosh, I look so bad in that one. I didn't know you were taking pictures at the airport this morning. You should have warned us."

"Too true. It's one thing to have ice cream for breakfast," said Lucy. "But having photographic proof that we had ice cream for breakfast is another thing entirely."

"And I have Chunky Monkey all over my face in that one," Ashlin cried.

Cameron squinted at the tiny image. "Um, I'm pretty sure that's a zit."

"Oh, great. That's so much better," Ashlin said. "Let me delete it, please?"

Cameron shook her head. "I don't want to erase anything until I see them on a bigger screen. I promise I'll get rid of anything unflattering."

"Can't you just do it now?" Ashlin begged.

"Okay, but just this one." Cameron reluctantly took the camera back and erased the shot.

Hadley reached for it next, saying, "I never saw the pictures from your graduation party. Can I take a look?"

Cameron put her camera back in its case. "They're all on my computer, at home."

"And they're all of her and Blake," Lucy added. "They're so cute, they seriously make me want to hurl."

Having recently been dumped—two days before the senior prom—and having vowed to hook up with no fewer than three random guys in Cabo, Lucy was on an antiboyfriend kick. Cameron understood where she was coming from, but that didn't make her comments any less annoying.

"All I have here are my shots from this morning," she said. "But I'll be taking a ton of pictures this week. I was hoping you guys would pose for me at the beach later."

"How come you're so camera-happy today?" asked Ashlin.

"She's always camera-happy. I mean, she just won the

annual photo award for, like, the third year running," Lucy pointed out.

"True, but school is out," said Hadley. "So what's the deal?"

Cameron explained, "I just found out that David Champlain is teaching a photo workshop at UCSB."

"Who?" asked Taylor.

"He's this amazing photographer who was on staff at *Vanity Fair* and he's also shot every cool ad you can think of—Prada, Guess, Louis Vuitton. Now he does art stuff. I saw an exhibit of his at the Museum of Contemporary Art, and I just found out that he's going to be teaching at UCSB. The problem is, this is a one-shot deal. He's only doing it for the first semester, and when I called the school so I could register, I found out that they have a really strict no-freshmen rule. So I figured I'd send my portfolio to him beforehand and beg."

"You'll get in, no problem," said Hadley.

"Yeah," Taylor agreed. "You always get whatever you want."

No one objected to this, and Cameron felt like the sun was shining on her and her alone. Even though she'd moved to Bel Air almost three years ago, she was still surprised, sometimes, that the beautiful people actually liked her.

Hadley dipped one foot into the pool. "Oh, it's cold. I thought the heat was on."

"It is," said Lucy as she stood up and retied the straps of her bikini top. "It takes a while to kick in, though. I'm going to take a walk on the beach. Anyone want to come?"

"I will," said Ashlin.

"Us too," said Hadley, answering, as usual, for both herself and Taylor.

Cameron looked toward the house. "I'll meet you guys out there. I want to call Blake first."

"Ha, I win," Taylor laughed as she hopped from one foot to the other.

"What?" asked Cameron, turning around.

"We placed bets on how long you'd be here before calling Blake," Lucy explained. "I thought you'd wait until tomorrow, at least."

"I knew it would be this afternoon," said Taylor. "I figured you'd want to call him as soon as the plane landed, but you knew we'd make fun of you for it. So you tried to draw it out as long as possible."

Cameron couldn't exactly object, since Taylor had called it pretty much on the nose.

As her friends filed down the cement steps to the beach, Cameron headed in the opposite direction, slipping through the sliding glass doors and into the house. Then she pulled her cell phone from her backpack, flopped down onto the white, overstuffed couch, and put her feet on the glass coffee table (something she'd never have been able to do if Lucy's parents had been there).

"Hey, cutie," she said to Blake as soon as he picked up the phone.

"Hi," he replied. "How is it down there?"

"Amazing," said Cameron. "It's so warm, and the beach is stunning."

"Rub it in, why don't you. I so wish I was there."

"I wish you were too."

"If your friends didn't have that 'no guys allowed' rule."

"It is our last time all together," said Cameron. "For a while, anyway."

"Tell me about it," said Blake.

Surprisingly, Cameron felt her eyes tear up. Not because she'd be separated from Blake for five days, but because this was essentially a sad preview to their real good-bye in the fall. Cameron was going to UC Santa Barbara in September, while Blake was on his way to UC Santa Cruz. Sure, they planned to stay together, but it wouldn't be the same, and they both knew it. The drive between the two schools was four and a half hours without traffic—and there was always traffic.

"We still have the summer," said Cameron.

"True, and I just heard back from the Joshua Tree people. We got a great camping spot. We'll be the first at the park to see the sunrise."

"Wait, why would we be up that early?"

Blake laughed. "You're gonna love it."

"Know what I love?" said Cameron. "Indoor plumbing. You really shouldn't underestimate it."

This was a game they sometimes played. Cameron acted like a high-maintenance heiress, while Blake played the rugged outdoorsy guy exasperated by his girlfriend's demands. Neither acknowledged that in many ways they genuinely *did* live up to the stereotypes they were mocking, because that would have spoiled the fun.

"Camping is awesome," said Blake. "Trust me."

"That's what you said about Leo Carillo, before our tent was invaded by ten thousand red ants."

"Oh, please. I only counted three."

"Three hundred you mean." Cameron sighed an exaggerated sigh. "Don't you know that for every single ant you see, there are a hundred more waiting in the wings?"

"Paranoid much?"

"I'm not making it up. It's a fact." Cameron was emphatic.

There was often an inverse relationship between what she insisted was true and the actual truth, but Blake knew better than to argue.

"Okay, fine," he relented. "There were three hundred ants. It could have been a lot worse, though. It could have been three hundred cockroaches."

"Gross!" yelled Cameron.

"All you needed was more time to adjust. Camping for one night doesn't really count."

"If it doesn't count, then why couldn't we go to Jake's Barefoot Bar for dinner? They make my favorite fish tacos on the planet and we were only eighteen miles away."

"You can't go to a restaurant when you're camping."

"Your logic is flawed," Cameron replied. "Because you already said it didn't count."

"Okay, fine. It's silly of me to argue with someone who's always right. I'll make it up to you. We'll go to Jake's as soon as you get back from Cabo. Straight from the airport, I promise. Now I've gotta run or I'll be late for work."

"Call me tomorrow," said Cameron. "And don't OD on garden burgers."

It was a necessary warning. Blake waited tables at the Banana Leaf Café, a vegetarian restaurant in Venice. When he worked, he was allowed to eat all he wanted for free, and more than once he'd come home stuffed to the gills and too sick to go out.

After hanging up, Cameron walked back to the master bedroom she was sharing with Lucy and turned on the shower. The cool, steady stream of water was a refreshing break from the hot sun, just as Cabo was a refreshing break from her regular life. Not that her regular life was so bad. After all, Cameron had a sweet, gorgeous, and totally devoted boyfriend, amazing friends, cool, lenient parents, and a sister who was maybe a tad dorky, but still very chill. Plus, she had an entire summer of freedom. All she had to worry about was working on her portfolio and maintaining her tan. The possibilities stretched endlessly before her, kind of like the vast Sea of Cortez, which she could see from the shower window.

Cameron was just stepping out of the stall when she heard Lucy burst into the room and announce, "You won't believe our luck. Totally hot guys at three o'clock."

"What?" Cameron wrapped a white, plush towel around her body and headed out of the bathroom.

Lucy stood in front of the mirror over the dresser, brushing out her hair. "You know how our neighbors rent out their house sometimes?" She pointed her brush to the left, presumably toward said neighbors' house.

Cameron shrugged. "Um, no."

"Well, they do," said Lucy. "And this week it's rented to a bunch of hot guys, and it's perfect because there are six of them. One for each of you and two for me. And don't you get all moral on me. Blake is in LA, which is a thousand miles from here. Plus, cheating when you're in a foreign country is technically not even cheating."

"I didn't realize." Sure, Cameron played it cool, but she couldn't ignore the flutter of curiosity this news brought. New guys were the best kind, so full of possibility.

Lucy egged her on. "Flirting isn't cheating. Enjoying yourself isn't cheating."

Not that Cameron needed to be convinced. "Fine," she said. "Just let me get dressed."

"Okay, but hurry up." Lucy started for the door but then paused and glanced over her shoulder. "So how come you never told me that the guys from La Jolla were so hot?"

"What?" Suddenly unsteady on her feet, Cameron grabbed the edge of the dressing table. While it seemed too dramatic a gesture, she couldn't help herself. She felt jolted whenever any reference was made to La Jolla, which reminded her of her former life: the one where she wasn't beautiful and popular, the one where she was in fact teased and ridiculed. It had been more than three years since then, but the pain was still raw.

"You heard me," said Lucy, staring at her curiously. "Take a look."

Cameron stepped out onto the balcony and saw a group of guys playing touch football on the beach down below.

"Can you believe how lucky we are?" Lucy followed her outside.

Cameron nodded silently. Lucy was right. The guys were cute, but that wasn't why she kept staring, and that wasn't why she suddenly had a very bitter taste in the back of her throat.

The problem was, Cameron knew these guys. Every single one of them. They were Braden, Emmett, Hunter, Devon, Max, and Travis, the very same people who had once made her life so miserable.

"Will you hurry up and get dressed?" said Lucy, nervously watching as Hadley and Taylor approached the guys.

Cameron didn't move. Nor did she say anything. She couldn't.

"Wait, what are you staring at?" asked Lucy. "See that one with dark hair and the goatee? He's mine. I also call the one with the shaggy blond hair. And the one with the short dark hair . . ."

Feeling quite suddenly like she'd woken up after a night of pounding tequila shots—which is to say, fuzzy-headed and on the verge of puking—Cameron walked back inside. She sat down on the edge of the bed.

"What's wrong with you?" asked Lucy, hands up in an exaggerated shrug.

"Nothing," Cameron whispered.

"Well, are you coming?"

"I think," said Cameron, flopping down onto her back and staring up at the ceiling, "I think I'm going to need a minute."

CHAPTER TWO

Allie Beekman had been told that Dr. Glass was many things: a top Beverly Hills plastic surgeon, the husband of super-model Venus Alder, and a virtual miracle worker. This was all very hard to believe, because to Allie he seemed like nothing more than a slick older man with a too-bright smile.

His office was full of leather and glass and shiny metal. There were sharp right angles everywhere, and there was nothing organic, nothing living or breathing, in the entire place except for Allie and her mom. She wasn't yet willing to grant Dr. Glass regular human-being status. His features were too chiseled, like the statue of David she'd seen in her art history textbook. Also, he wore his shirt unbuttoned too far, exposing a tan chest that seemed surprisingly smooth for someone his age.

The fish in the tank behind Dr. Glass were floating belly-up on the water's surface. For Allie, this did not inspire confidence.

Not even after she realized that the fish were plastic, and that it was a joke. Postmodern, probably. At least that's what Cameron would say, although Allie wasn't entirely sure why.

Her opinion of the doctor did not matter, though, since no one had asked her for it.

"I just want to make sure it's natural-looking," said Julie, Allie's mom, for the third time in fifteen minutes.

"Of course," Dr. Glass replied, as if it were the easiest thing in the world. And perhaps for him, it was. "I'll give her a nose that fits her face."

"I hate noses that look like they were done," Julie continued. "I don't want people to look at her and think, *nose job*."

Then why am I getting one in the first place? Allie wondered, but only to herself.

"You've nothing to worry about, Ms. Davenport." Dr. Glass flashed his blinding white smile. "Your daughter is in excellent hands."

Allie looked down at the doctor's hands and cringed.

"I'm sure you have these on file, but I brought pictures of my older daughter, Cameron." Julie pulled a stack of photos from her purse and handed them to Dr. Glass. "You probably don't remember, but you fixed her nose three years ago."

"Of course I remember." Dr. Glass glanced at the top picture for a millisecond before handing them all back. "How's Cameron doing these days?"

"Wonderful," said Julie, her blue eyes lighting up. "She just graduated from Bel Air Prep and she's on her way to UC Santa Barbara."

"Fantastic," said Dr. Glass.

"She also got into UPenn," said Julie. "But she has her heart set on staying in Southern California."

Allie rolled her eyes. Her mother told everyone that Cameron also got into Penn. She seriously doubted that Dr. Glass cared, or that he even remembered her. Before she came in, Allie had done some research, so she knew that besides nose jobs—rhinoplasty, to get technical—he also did breast and chin and cheek and pectoral and calf implants and face-lifts and eye tucks and tummy tucks and liposuction and Botox. Her mother had booked Allie's appointment four months in advance. Dr. Glass was *that* busy. So how many noses had he done, she wondered, since her sister's? If he did three a week, working for fifty weeks a year, that added up to a hundred and fifty noses. Times three years equaled four hundred and fifty.

"So she's smart *and* beautiful."

"Yes, thanks to you." Julie smiled as if Dr. Glass had performed the surgery out of the goodness of his heart, rather than for his normal fee of eight thousand dollars. (Allie had looked that up too.)

"That's why we came back to you for Allie," her mother continued. "We're hoping you can do the same for her."

"I do a lot of families and it's always an honor," said Dr. Glass. "Now do you have any more questions?"

"Yes," said Julie. "Aren't you going to show us how she'll look after the surgery? When we came with Cameron, we got to see her altered image on a computer."

Dr. Glass frowned for the first time. "The digital-imaging machine is broken. But you can come back next week so you'll know what you're getting."

"Oh, good," said Julie. "We'd definitely like to see."

"By the way," said Dr. Glass. "I caught *The Deepest Bluest Sea* on HBO last night. Your performance was magnificent. It had my wife in tears."

"Thanks." Julie tucked her blond hair behind her ears and cast her gaze downward. "That was a long time ago."

Allie never ceased to be surprised by her mom's bashfulness. Before she had kids, Julie had been a well-known actress. She'd even been nominated for an Academy Award once. Yet whenever anyone mentioned it, she acted like she wished they hadn't.

"Well, I don't want to keep you two." Dr. Glass stood up.

"Will it hurt?" Allie asked quickly. It was her first question, the first time she'd spoken since they arrived.

"You'll be under anesthesia," said Dr. Glass, waving his hand to dismiss the thought. "You won't feel a thing."

"But what about after?" asked Allie. "Will it hurt then?"

"You may feel woozy from being under for so long."

"How long?"

"Two hours, maybe, but you'll never know it. You'll come in here at seven thirty and you'll walk out by eleven."

"There are no side effects, then?"

"No. The splint will come off in four or five days, and in three weeks the major swelling will go down and you'll be as good as new. Well, mostly. You'll be slightly swollen for six months to a year after, but that's minimal." Dr. Glass smiled. "You'll hardly notice."

"Three weeks?" Allie glanced at her mother, worriedly. "But I'm supposed to go to soccer camp on July thirtieth."

"That's up to the doctor, dear," Julie said.

Looking down at his calendar, Dr. Glass shook his head. "That's only two weeks after your surgery day, so no, I wouldn't recommend it. Your nose will be too fragile at that point. If you get hit in the face with the ball, it could break all over again. We'd have to start over from scratch."

"The whole team is going to Colorado," said Allie. "I have to be there."

"Isn't the camp three weeks long?" asked Julie. "Maybe you can go late."

"Or perhaps we can fit you in sooner," said Dr. Glass. "Why don't you speak with Madison, my patient coordinator, on the way out?"

"Thank you, Dr. Glass," Julie gushed as she stood up. "We'll do that."

"I have one more question," said Allie, turning in the doorway. "What if I don't like it?"

"Like what?" asked Dr. Glass.

"My new nose."

Dr. Glass tilted his head to one side and looked at her, really looked at *her*, and not just her nose or her mother, for the first time. "What do you mean?"

He seemed truly perplexed.

Allie felt her cheeks heat up. Still, she had to ask, "Um, can you put it back to how it was, if I don't like it?"

Julie interrupted her. "Allie, don't be silly. You'll love your new nose."

"Trust me," said Dr. Glass. "I've been doing this for a very long time. You have nothing to worry about."

"We trust you," said Julie as she put her arm around Allie and steered her out the door.

Back in the waiting room they spoke to Madison. "You're getting rhinoplasty?" she asked before she even looked at Allie's chart.

Julie answered for her. "Yes, she is."

Allie wished the floor would open up and swallow her whole. Was it that obvious? Sure, her nose was large, but did that mean everyone looked at it and thought, *That girl needs surgery?*

"Don't worry. Dr. Glass does amazing work." Madison stretched out the word "amazing" as if she were describing the chocolate soufflé at the Four Seasons. "You'll love him."

It was then that Allie noticed Madison's breasts, which were spilling out of her top. They seemed too big to be real. Was this the work of Dr. Glass? And did Madison get a discount? she wondered. Or was she working off the cost?

"We were hoping that Dr. Glass could fit Allie in earlier," said Julie. "Perhaps if he has something next week. Or even later this week . . ."

"You're in a hurry, huh?" Madison asked.

"It's not that," said Allie. "It's just . . . I have other stuff I want to do this summer."

Madison nodded, as if either she didn't care or she didn't believe her. She looked at her computer screen, typing quickly with slender, manicured hands. "Oh, sorry, but he's fully booked. Summer is a busy time—especially for noses. You know, with school out and everything. Tell you what, though. I'll put you on the waiting list. Anything opens up and I'll give you a call, okay, honey?" Madison winked at her.

"Thanks," said Julie. "We appreciate that."

Allie couldn't decide what she despised more, being called honey or being winked at.

Once they were in the elevator, her mom turned to her. "I know how important soccer is to you, Allie, but in the long run you'll be happy you did this."

Her mom looked so hopeful, so excited about the whole thing, that Allie didn't want to disappoint her. "I guess it's just a week," she said with a shrug.

Allie couldn't stay mad at her mom, who was only doing what she thought was best. Julie always did what she thought was best. That's why she'd given up acting after she had kids. That's why she drove car pool and that's why she went to all of Allie's soccer games, always bringing orange wedges and Gatorade for the whole team.

"I'm sure something will open up," Julie continued. "Just in case it doesn't, though, I'll check with the airline to see if we can push your departure date back by a week or two. And you should call Coach McAdams to let her know you may not make it."

"Okay." Allie squinted as they stepped into the bright sunshine of West LA.

It was lunchtime and the sidewalk swelled with men and women. Most wore suits and they all walked quickly, rushing to important places. Half of them had cell phones stuck to their ears. Dr. Glass's building—the "surgi-center," he called it on his website—seemed discreet. Blending in with the surrounding glass and concrete buildings, it could easily be mistaken for a bank or an insurance office. Yet Allie still felt embarrassed leaving, as if everyone knew what really went on at that address.

"Do you want to drive home?" asked Julie, handing over the keys to the car.

She must really feel bad, Allie realized. She'd only gotten her permit last month, and all of her driving lessons so far had been with her dad.

"Are you sure?" Allie stared at her mom's car, a large navy blue BMW, warily. She didn't want to drive it but couldn't think of a plausible excuse not to.

"Your dad said you're doing very well," Julie replied. "So why not?"

It was one thing to do well in empty parking lots and on traffic-free streets just after sunrise. Driving in afternoon traffic was another thing entirely, but it seemed silly to mention this. It was only driving. Allie would have to figure it out eventually.

Taking the keys, she opened the door and slid into the driver's seat. Allie was used to her dad's tiny sports car. Her mom's four-door sedan felt like a whole different category of vehicle—closer to an ocean liner than a car. But Allie refused to complain or even comment. She could tell she'd already put a damper on her mom's plans, what with asking silly questions of Dr. Glass and worrying about missing camp. He was a top Beverly Hills surgeon. Why would he care about her soccer schedule? How could she have expressed doubt that she'd love his work? His wife radiated beauty, as did his secretary. All of the actresses rumored to be his clients (according to her mom and her sister) were also stunning. Cameron looked amazing, and she'd probably done much better during her consultation. Cameron always did things better.

After adjusting the seat and mirrors, buckling her seat belt, and checking to see that her mom was ready, Allie carefully backed out of the parking space onto busy Wilshire Boulevard.

"Nice work." Julie nodded. "Now turn left at the light up here, and don't forget to signal."

Allie exhaled after she made the turn.

They weren't too far from home. Allie focused on the road and tried not to think about the surgery, how she'd read that the doctor would have to cut across the bottom of her nose and peel the skin back, then break the bone to put it in its new place.

Her mom's cell phone rang, interrupting Allie's gruesome thoughts.

"Hello?" Julie asked. "Oh hi, Peter. Hold on a second." She cupped the mouthpiece of the phone with one hand and turned to Allie. "You're doing great, Allie. Why don't you turn right at the light? There'll be less traffic if we go the back way."

"Okay." Allie checked her rearview mirror three times and then glanced over her shoulder before changing lanes. The mere mention of traffic caused her shoulders to tense. The steering on the BMW was different, more stiff than what she was used to. Allie had to pull on the wheel harder to turn, coming dangerously close to the cars parked on the side of the road. At least she thought she came dangerously close. Her mom didn't say anything, so maybe she was doing okay.

Julie spoke into the phone. "I was just thinking about you . . . No? Did they say why? Oh. Well, no, that's okay . . ."

Allie couldn't help but eavesdrop. She knew her mom had been up for a role in some new movie. With Cameron on her way to college and Allie a soon-to-be-licensed driver, Julie had decided to go back to work. Although in her industry other people decided whether or not they wanted you back.

Peter O'Reilly was her new agent at ICM, and she'd just started auditioning two weeks before. Clearly, she hadn't gotten the part. Allie felt bad. Her mom had been excited about it and had said she thought the audition went well.

She glanced at her mom, and then immediately saw something small and brown dart into the road.

Allie swerved without even thinking.

It happened faster than a blink. The next thing she knew, a horrible sound filled her ears: glass shattering, metal scraping against metal, crunching and grinding.

When she realized what was happening Allie screamed and slammed on the brakes. But it was too late.

Her mom turned to her and asked, "Are you okay? Tell me you're okay."

Allie was okay, yet too upset to say so. She was shaking and could hear herself breathing heavily.

Her mom seemed fine, although shocked. Julie was clutching her phone so hard, her knuckles had turned bone white. Allie was surprised the phone didn't splinter into pieces. "I'm going to have to call you back," Julie said.

Glancing down at herself, Allie half expected to see blood,

yet her T-shirt was clean, which made her feel silly. Sure, she'd been jolted, but big deal. No one was hurt, so why was her body shaking uncontrollably?

When Allie looked in the rearview mirror, her heart sank to her knees. The car behind her seemed damaged, pushed in.

"Tell me you're okay," Julie repeated.

Allie opened up her mouth and felt something tickle the back of her throat. She couldn't speak, so instead she burst into tears.

CHAPTER THREE

"You are such a freak show sometimes," Lucy called as she headed downstairs. "I'm outta here." Her tone was as clear as the cloudless sky. *I'm sort of joking,* it said, *but not really.*

Cameron didn't blame Lucy for being perplexed. If the guys on the beach had been anyone other than her former tormentors, she'd be scrambling to get dressed and out the door. But the situation was much more complicated. As far as her friends were concerned, she'd always been the Cameron they knew and loved: smart, beautiful, and carefree. In her invented past, the one she'd told them about, life had never been a struggle. And for three years it had been so easy to pretend that this image had been genuine, her only true self. At least it had been until now, when her past appeared right in front of her, playing football on the beach less than twenty yards away.

On one level, she knew she was being overly dramatic. The

world had larger problems—war, famine, and the proliferation of Hooters across America, to name a few. (Any guy who said he ate there for the excellent barbeque was lying through his teeth.) But that didn't take away from the fact that Cameron had been miserable for four long years, tormented mercilessly from the sixth through the ninth grade. She didn't want to remember, yet the pain remained in the pit of her stomach, like a balled-up fist that refused to unclench.

When she finally peeled herself off the bed, she slipped into her favorite pink bikini, which was slightly padded but didn't look it, and headed back to the balcony. The football game had broken up. Lucy was talking to all three of the guys she'd claimed: Hunter, Max, and Braden. They were certainly less scrawny than Cameron remembered. They'd gone through other changes, too—Hunter had graduated from a bowl cut to a buzz, Braden now stood a head taller than his friends, and Max sported stubble that was visible from the balcony—but they were still the same guys. Cameron would have recognized them from a mile away.

And here were her best friends flirting with the enemy.

Lucy tossed her hair and laughed her exaggerated *look at me* laugh. Hadley and Taylor were both captivated by Travis, a surfer with shoulder-length dark hair and piercing blue eyes. Ashlin threw a Frisbee with the remaining two, Emmett and Devon.

Back in junior high, those guys seemed like movie stars.

They inhabited their own fabulous and very distant universe. Cameron hadn't thought about them for a long time. She hadn't needed to.

Taking a deep breath, Cameron steeled herself against her fears. No way would the guys recognize her. She was an entirely different person. So why did she feel like crawling into bed and pulling the covers up over her head?

Things were different and she needed to prove it, so she headed to the bathroom, where her hair dryer awaited.

Twenty minutes later Cameron strutted onto the beach, still in the pink bikini, with a bright green sarong slung low around her hips. Her long hair hung loose down her back. She batted her mascara-coated eyelashes, pulled her cherry-tinted lips into a smile, and walked like she had something to prove.

"What took you so long?" Lucy asked.

Cameron smiled and projected her voice. "Well, I was dripping wet and *naked* when you found me. What did you expect?"

Upon hearing the word "naked," all six guys looked at Cameron. Including Devon, even though a Frisbee was sailing toward his head.

A second later, it clocked him in the face. Everyone laughed, except for Cameron, who flashed a self-satisfied smile.

"I made a pitcher of strawberry margaritas," she called to the crowd. "Anyone thirsty?"

A smiling, bikini-clad blonde offering free alcohol: that was all it took for the six guys to follow Cameron back into the house. And where the guys went, her friends followed.

"Who wants salt?" Cameron asked as she headed to the outdoor bar where she'd set everything up, the blender, ice, tequila, and glasses arranged almost as carefully as her plans for the La Jolla guys.

Hunter, Braden, and Max did. Emmett and Travis didn't. And Devon was too busy icing the bruise over his eye (with the help of Ashlin) to be paying any attention to the drink orders.

Lucy went inside to get the chips and salsa.

"There's beer, too," said Hadley, pulling a six-pack of Corona from the outdoor minifridge.

Everyone else settled onto the lawn furniture at the far end of the pool.

"Our lucky day," said Travis, grinning at Cameron.

Lucky day, she thought bitterly. When we were partners in seventh-grade science class, you did everything you could to get away from me. Even though I did all the work and got us an A.

She walked across the patio and sat down between Braden and Hunter. "I don't think we've met," she said. "I'm Cammi."

Thankfully, her friends were too busy flirting to notice her brand-new nickname. So afraid of being recognized, Cameron had even lowered her voice an octave.

"Hey, nice to meet you," said Braden.

(This from a guy who'd once tripped her in the hallway.)

"Excellent margaritas," said Hunter, who used to stick gum in her hair on a weekly basis.

"They always taste better down here. Don't you think?" asked Cameron.

"Don't know," Hunter replied. "I've never been to Mexico before. But I can tell you one thing, they taste much better when I'm sitting next to a really cute girl."

Cameron forced a smile and pretended the line wasn't horribly pathetic. "You're too sweet," she lied.

"We need some music," Hadley called from across the room.

"Totally," Taylor agreed.

Cameron slapped her hand against her forehead. "I had my Phish CDs out to pack, but I totally spaced."

"I love Phish," said Braden, scrambling to his feet. "I have some great bootlegs back at our place. I'll go get them."

"Excellent," said Cameron.

Lucy glanced at her, confused. Probably because she knew Cameron didn't have any Phish CDs. Why would she when she hated the band so much? (Blake thought Trey Anastasio was a musical genius. Cameron thought he was a Jerry Garcia wannabe. It was one of the few things they fought about.)

She grinned at Lucy, who let it pass. Cameron knew she'd have to come up with some sort of explanation later, but there were other things to focus on now. Like, for instance, the following fact: Now that Braden had taken off, there was plenty of space on the couch, but neither Cameron nor Hunter had moved. In fact, their bare knees kissed.

She reached for her own drink and took a sip. It was icy cold and just sweet enough to overpower the tequila.

"So, where are you going next year?" asked Cameron.

"San Diego State," Hunter replied.

"Sounds like fun." Cameron drained her drink.

"That's the plan."

Cameron poured herself another margarita and topped off Hunter's. The booze and mindless conversation flowed freely. Soon they were giggly and drunk. Everyone was. *It's that easy,* thought Cameron. She was in. Hanging out with the same guys who used to avert their eyes when she passed them in the hall. Now they watched her. And it wasn't to see if she messed up so they'd have more ammunition. No, they'd been fooled. They actually thought she was one of them. It was such a rush. Better even than her first few months of tenth grade, when her popularity fit her like a stylish, yet too-stiff-to-be-comfortable, new coat.

Her plan had been to flirt relentlessly with the La Jolla guys and then reveal her true self and send them all packing. But this was too much fun. She'd feared these guys for so long. In a sick way, she'd envied and almost worshiped them too. Yet now, three years later, they seemed so ordinary.

Someone must have turned on the radio, because Bob Marley blared from the outdoor speakers.

Ashlin and Devon were getting very cozy at one end of the pool. Lucy was, for some reason, petting Max's head. And everyone else was getting into the hot tub.

Cameron didn't even hear anyone approach, so she was surprised to turn around and find Braden. He had the bootlegs with him, and somebody else. Some *bodies*, that is, the sight of which caused Cameron to choke on her drink.

Trailing behind Braden were three more of her classmates from La Jolla: Keisha, Nikki, and Alexis.

The La Jolla guys' teasing had always been harsh, but that was nothing compared to the girls'. They'd been unmerciful. Especially Alexis and Nikki, who had not once but twice cut Cameron's bra in half while she was showering after gym class. (They'd claimed she was too flat to wear one. Sadly, this was still the case.)

The chilling looks, the blatant laughter, the unrelenting cruelty—it all came flooding back to Cameron at the very sight of these people.

"There you are," said Alexis, striding past Cameron without even acknowledging her existence. She leaned toward Hunter and kissed him on the lips. "We got to the house and it was empty, and we were like, 'Where are they?' And then Braden comes in, and I'm like, 'Where is everyone else?' So he brought me here. Are you guys ready? Because I was about to order pizza."

The three girls from La Jolla surveyed Cameron's friends and the entire scene.

Nikki's cold eyes seemed to linger for too long on Cameron.

You're so unbalanced. You've got that huge nose and such a flat chest, she'd once said. *It's really sad.*

Suddenly, Cameron had the chills. She crossed her arms over her chest, self-conscious for the first time all day, hating that these girls still had the power to make her feel so small.

"So you guys are renting a house this week too?" asked Keisha, finally acknowledging Cameron and her friends.

"No, this is my parents' place," said Lucy.

No one said anything. And even though it was eighty-five degrees outside, the air felt as chilly as early morning on a winter day.

Cameron meant to set her margarita on the coffee table but missed. It tipped over and the remaining red liquid spilled to the ground.

"Shit!" yelled Lucy, getting up and running to the kitchen for a towel.

"Sorry," said Cameron, watching as the stain spread out over the terra-cotta tile. It wasn't as if there would be permanent damage, but it still felt humiliating.

Leave it to Ashlin to try and make friends. "Anyone want a drink?" she asked. "The margaritas are amazing. They're totally the Platonic ideal."

Nikki glanced at Ashlin quizzically. "What are you talking about?"

"Just nod and go along with whatever she says," Hadley advised. "That's what we do when she talks about Roman philosophers."

"Greek," Ashlin corrected her.

Hadley flipped her hair over her shoulder. "Whatever."

Alexis, never a shy one, shrugged and said, "Okay. I'll have a Corona."

"Me too," said Keisha.

Nikki helped herself to a margarita. "Platon was right," she said. "These are delicious."

Lucy came back with a wet dishcloth and tossed it to Cameron.

Suddenly, everything was normal. They were just hanging out, talking, and even laughing. Cameron soaked up the drink. Watching the redness seep into the white rag, she tried to pretend these girls were strangers. *You can do this,* she said to herself, but not very convincingly. Her hands were shaking, and she noticed a chip in her nail polish. Suddenly the padding in her bathing suit top seemed way too obvious. Was Nikki still staring at her? Cameron peeked and then quickly looked away. Nikki *was* still staring.

Braden sat down next to her and started talking about some Phish reunion tour that was just so awesome. Cameron pretended to be interested, all the while focused, peripherally, on the La Jolla girls' moves. She didn't trust them, and she didn't trust herself around them.

After a while, Nikki said to Cameron, "You look so familiar."

Lucy overheard this and said, "Cameron is from La Jolla. Where did you go to school before you transferred to Bel Air?"

Cameron had no choice but to admit the truth. "I went to Country Day."

"That's where we went," said Keisha.

"Wait," said Max. "I thought you said you just graduated high school."

"I did."

"So you were in our grade?" asked Braden.

Cameron nodded, happy that none of the kids recognized her.

"But our school isn't even that big. What's your last name?" asked Keisha.

It was ironic that Keisha was the one to blow her cover. Of all the La Jolla girls, Keisha had been the least cruel back then. Sometimes she was even nice (although at the time Cameron had figured this was out of pity).

Reluctantly, Cameron admitted, "Beekman."

All conversation ceased. It was so quiet that Cameron heard a seal calling in the distance, as if even the animals in the ocean were stunned by the revelation.

The La Jolla crowd looked uniformly shocked, while Cameron's Bel Air friends were just confused.

"Oh my gosh," said Alexis. "You're Beakface!" She couldn't have been drunk already, but she sure was acting that way.

"Cammi. Wait, you're Cameron Beekman?" asked Braden, inching away as if she were diseased.

"There's no way." Devon gasped.

Hunter and Max stared at her. They all did.

"Yes, she's Cameron Beekman," said Nikki, setting down her margarita as if it were poisoned. "I knew it!"

"Weren't you a brunette?" asked Alexis.

Cameron shrugged, not denying it.

As Taylor looked back and forth between the La Jolla crowd and Cameron, her blond pigtails swung. "You know one another?" she asked.

"Kind of," said Cameron.

"I mean, I never would have recognized you. Not in a million. Not in a gazillion trillion years," said Nikki.

Cameron was glad she was unrecognizable, but at the same time she felt insulted. So she'd had a big nose and braces . . . Nikki was treating her like she'd been the Bride of Frankenstein.

Yet why did she even care what these people thought of her? She despised them.

Still, she'd enjoyed flirting with Hunter. Knowing she *could* flirt with Hunter. What was wrong with her?

Alexis turned to Cameron and said, "What, did you get a nose job or something?"

Way to thrust the knife in even deeper, thought Cameron, now too mortified to speak.

She couldn't lie. She could try, but no way would they believe her.

She shrugged, again. They'd reduced her to practically a mute in just a few minutes. It was like seventh grade all over again. "Um, I guess," she said.

"You guess?" Alexis laughed, cruelly. "I didn't know there was any guessing involved. Either you had one or you didn't."

"I—," Cameron began.

"It's okay. You look great. I never would have recognized you," said Braden.

"I know. Huge improvement," Keisha added.

It felt like charity, and charity was the last thing Cameron wanted.

"We have stuff to do," said Lucy, interrupting, sitting down next to Cameron. "So if no one wants anything else . . ."

Everyone wanted something else, but Lucy wasn't really offering. The guys and girls from La Jolla ripped their scrutinizing gazes from Cameron and set their drinks down. Everyone who was in the hot tub got out. No one even asked for towels.

"Um, thanks," said Hunter, taking one last look behind him as they filed out.

Cameron gulped down her third margarita, walked inside

and collapsed on the living room couch. The room was spinning. Or maybe it was just her head.

Sure, she'd had a nose job, but that was only a small part of her transformation. Cameron was a whole different person. She'd just proved it.

Braden had jumped at her simple request for new music. Hunter, apparently Alexis's boyfriend, had had his arm around her. Their knees had rested casually against each other . . .

So why had she allowed these girls to get to her? Why did her confidence drain at lightning speed?

Cameron could answer her own questions. It wasn't just that the pain was so raw. In the back of her mind, she'd always wondered how much her nose had to do with her success at Bel Air Prep. She'd often played a game with herself, trying to imagine what her life would have been like under different circumstances: If she'd gotten the nose job but hadn't transferred schools, if she hadn't gotten the nose job and had transferred . . .

Was her current social status based on a lie? Would she even have her current friends if it weren't for her new nose? Or was it all about the plastic surgery, the eight-thousand-dollar investment her parents had made to fix her face? The problem was, this made her feel like a fraud. It was like cheating on a big exam and getting an A. Sure, the result is great, but you can never truly be happy with yourself, knowing how you got it.

"They're horrible," said Hadley.

"I know," Taylor agreed. "What bitches."

"And that guy Emmett?" said Ashlin. "He's only going to junior college."

Lucy, who had remained silent until now, looked out toward the beach and then back at Cameron. "So, Cammi," she said. "Tell us about Beakface."

CHAPTER FOUR

When it became clear that Allie was not going to calm down anytime soon, Julie got out of the car and walked around to the driver's side. Opening the door, she reached down and put her arms around her daughter's small, trembling body. "Don't worry, sweetie. No one was hurt, and it's just a car. We'll get it fixed."

Allie opened her mouth in a struggle to say something, anything, but she was too upset. Her throat had constricted to the point where speaking had become physically impossible. Even her breathing seemed labored.

"It was my fault," said Julie. "I never should have taken that call. I should have been paying closer attention, but you were doing so well. If that squirrel hadn't darted out into the road . . ."

So it was a squirrel she'd avoided and not a dog. This somehow made it worse. Not that Allie's thunderstorm of tears was really about animals or wrecked cars.

"Learning to drive takes time," Julie continued.

Allie pressed her fingertips to her closed eyes but was unable to block out the too smooth and smiling Dr. Glass.

The whole morning had been nightmarish. This accident should have been the climax—the final jolt to wake her up and make her realize she was safe in her bed at home, that none of this was real. But it wasn't happening.

No one had even asked her if she wanted a nose job. They'd just made all these plans around her, like she didn't even have a say in the matter. It was like when she was six and her mom signed her up for ballet class because Cameron had loved to dance.

Allie hated pink leotards.

And she'd just wrecked her mom's car.

Some stranger's car too.

When she hadn't even wanted to drive her mother's stupid boat of a car in the first place.

Everyone told Allie that she'd love to drive, but she wasn't convinced.

Here is what Allie loved: the smell of fresh, dewy grass early in the morning and the bold yellow and blue stripes on her soccer uniform. Also, the way her legs looked after practice—the red indentations on her skin from the straps of her shin guards and her tight socks, the flecks of dried mud that stuck to her knees.

Her team went to Colorado every summer because training

in the high altitude made them stronger. Allie had been longing for the cool mountain air ever since she'd had to leave it last summer. At soccer camp, all anyone talked about was the game for three weeks straight.

Allie didn't want to miss a minute of it. Not even for a better nose.

And that wasn't all. It was mortifying to sit there while her mother showed the surgeon pictures of her sister. To Allie, Julie's message was clear: "Cameron is our perfect, beautiful daughter. We would like for Allie to be just like her."

Allie wasn't like Cameron and she never would be. In all honesty, she didn't even strive to be. Between blowing out her hair, applying makeup, and getting dressed, it took Cameron ninety minutes to get ready for school every morning. Ninety minutes when they had to wear a uniform. Cameron agonized over her shoes and accessories, and it was all so much work. Allie didn't see the point.

Of course, explaining this to her mother was too complicated. Plus, her mom worried about stuff like that too, and Allie didn't want to insult her.

"Come look," said Julie, walking over to the wrecked car, a bright yellow Hummer, which was parked a few feet behind them. "It's not so bad, Allie. Really, it's not. This is why we have insurance."

Allie got out of the car and walked around to the other side. Her mom's car had a thick yellow scrape on the front bumper. The mirror on the passenger side had shattered, and the cracked chunk of plastic was dangling from the car by two measly wires. The Hummer was bashed in on one side, with the backseat door completely caved in.

The sight of it caused Allie's chest to tighten. The Hummer was designed for military purposes, to weather bullets and bombs and to be virtually indestructible. It was just like Allie to have found a way to destroy one with her mother's sedan. On a suburban street. In broad daylight.

"You'll feel better once you're home," said Julie. She pulled a scrap of paper and a pen from her purse and leaned against the Hummer's windshield to write. "I'll just leave a note for the owner of this car and we'll be off."

Allie sniffed and wiped her tears from her face with the back of her hand.

It was that simple. Her mom took care of everything, as usual.

"Thank God your face is okay," said Julie, once she was behind the wheel. "Did I ever tell you about my friend Mindy Davidson?"

Allie nodded. Julie told this story often. Allie knew it well; she also knew that once her mother got started, there was no stopping her.

"She was one of my first roommates in New York, back when I'd just been signed by the Ford Modeling Agency. We both moved to the city at around the same time, and we were both from small towns in Wisconsin. Eighteen years old, our first time living away from home—we had so much in common," Julie went on. "But she always did so much better than me—not that I minded. I was just happy to be away from home. Anyway, Mindy was spectacular. If it wasn't for the accident, I know she'd have been a huge success. She'd recently landed the cover of *Marie Claire*, and she was coming home late one night from a bar, in the rain, when her cab smashed into a brick wall. It was horrible. She broke every bone in her face, had to get emergency surgery. A top plastic surgeon saw her soon after, but it was too late. Even though he put her face back together again, something was lost."

Her mom always ended the story there, but to Allie it seemed incomplete. "What happened to her?" she asked.

"I told you. She never looked the same so she never worked again." Julie clucked her tongue and shook her head.

"At all?"

"In the industry." Her mom replied as if it were obvious, as if this were just one more dumb question that Allie shouldn't have had to ask. She opened the garage door. "You must still be upset. Please don't worry so much, Allie. Accidents happen."

Allie was glad that Cameron was still in Cabo. Getting into a car accident before she even had her license seemed too dorky, even for her. Allie couldn't bear to see the disappointment on her sister's face, the silent acknowledgment that there was something wrong with her. She'd read that look in her big sister's eyes when the homecoming court nominations came out last fall. Cameron had been nominated for the third year in a row, and Allie had not. Her big sister told her she'd been robbed, and Allie laughed. Not only had she not been expecting to be nominated, she hadn't even realized it was something she was supposed to want. The homecoming court didn't *do* anything. They just stood there on stage, smiling vacantly and wearing stupid plastic tiaras.

"Can we not tell Cameron about this?" Allie asked. "Please?"

"This isn't a big deal, Allie. Really, but if it's important to you, then don't worry. We'll just say the car needed to be serviced."

"Thank you."

"Please don't be so hard on yourself. This could have happened to anyone."

Maybe this was true, but the fact remained: It had happened to Allie. Things always happened to Allie.

On their first day of Bel Air Prep, Cameron had come home with a new best friend, while Allie had come home with a bee sting on her ear. Cameron got almost all As and Allie had to see a math tutor twice a week to maintain her B-minus. Cameron went out with Blake, who everyone loved, and Allie had never even kissed a guy.

As she headed for the stairs, her mom said, "Don't forget to call Coach McAdams."

"I won't," called Allie, as she headed for Cameron's room because that's where she could find the biggest mirror.

Once there she stared at herself. Allie had a good body from playing sports. Or at least, that's what everyone said, so she guessed it was true. Her smile was pretty as well. Her teeth were straight, and she'd never even needed braces. From the front her nose looked okay, but in profile it was on the large side. Still, it wasn't like it dominated her face. She had nice blue eyes and shiny, shoulder-length dark hair. It was all one length because Cameron had told her it looked better that way. She had a cute sprinkling of freckles across the bridge of her nose, and she wondered what would happen to them after the surgery. Would her freckles be in a different place? She wanted to ask but knew she couldn't without sounding dumb.

Allie headed back to her room, dreading the phone call she had to make. Sitting down cross-legged on her bed, she dialed her coach's number.

"Hello, Coach McAdams? This is Allie Beekman. I have to come to camp late this year, I think."

"Oh, hi, Allie. What do you mean, late?"

"Well, I can't come until August sixth," Allie admitted, as she pulled a loose thread from her sock.

"You'll be missing an entire week."

"I know."

"How is our team supposed to be prepared for the season

if I have players skipping half the camp?" asked Coach McAdams.

It's not really "players," thought Allie. *It's just me. And it's not half, only a third.* "I'm sorry. I really wish I could be there."

The coach sighed. Allie sensed that she was growing impatient. Coach McAdams lived and breathed soccer. She'd played in college and had almost made the US women's team in the 2004 Olympics. She'd even founded a soccer clinic for underprivileged kids. Allie's best friend, Quincy, was working there for the summer. Allie had wanted to as well, but she couldn't commit the time because of her surgery. Not that she'd used this excuse when she'd had to say no. Of course, now there was no avoiding it.

"You'll need to give me a reason, Allie."

She had to come clean, but it was so embarrassing. She took a deep breath and blurted out the news. "I'm getting a nose job in a few weeks, and the doctor says I can't play sports for three weeks after."

The coach was silent for a few moments. Allie felt her face burn red.

"Next year is going to be tough, Allie. I was really counting on you."

Allie cringed at her coach's use of the past tense. "I'll train extra hard once I recover."

"And I was going to wait until we were in Colorado to tell you this, but I have one spot left on the varsity team."

"Really?" asked Allie.

"Yes, Rachel Meyers is moving to Washington. That means I'll be pulling someone up from JV. Tryouts will be held on the last day of camp, and I could really use a left-footed forward on the team."

"Well, I'll be there in time," said Allie. "I'd love to play varsity next year."

"Sorry," said Coach McAdams. "If you're not going to camp for the entire three weeks, I can't give you a shot. It wouldn't be fair to everyone else."

Coach McAdams didn't need to voice the real issue. Allie knew what was at stake. She and Quincy were the stars of the JV team. Allie was left-footed, which gave her a slight advantage over Quincy, who was a more aggressive scorer. It would still be a lot of work to beat her, but if Allie didn't try out, then Quincy would be a shoo-in for the varsity team.

"Is there any other way?" asked Allie. "Maybe if I trained extra hard before and after?"

"I hate to come down so hard," said Coach McAdams. "You're a very valuable player. But this is the third plastic surgery-related phone call I've gotten this summer. There are already two sophomores leaving the team completely."

"Who else called?" Allie wondered.

"I'm not going to say," said the coach. "I need to respect their privacy. But I'll tell you this. It's no one on the starting team. You're the one I'm worried about losing."

"It wasn't even my idea. I'm on the waiting list for an earlier appointment, so there's a chance I can still make it."

"Well, let me know as soon as you figure that out," said the coach. "Okay?"

"I'm really sorry."

"So am I."

As soon as Allie hung up the phone, it rang again. She reached for it, hoping it was Coach McAdams changing her mind.

"Hello?" she asked.

"This is Brian Hughes. I'm calling about my Hummer."

"Oh, hi." Allie felt her heart sink. "It's my fault and I'm really, really sorry I wrecked it."

It was an afternoon of apologies.

"You're sorry?" He laughed a hostile laugh. "Let me ask you something, because I can't figure this out. There wasn't even another car parked on the entire street, so were you *trying* to hit my jeep?"

"No." Allie closed her eyes. "I haven't been driving for that long. It was an accident. Well, obviously. We'll pay for whatever damage." She felt her voice waver.

"Yeah, no shit."

Well, he didn't have to be so mean about it. Allie couldn't deal. "Hold on," she said. "Let me get my mother."

She ran to the head of the stairs and called, "Mom? The guy with the Hummer is on the phone."

"Hello, this is Julie Davenport," said Allie's mom, picking up immediately. "My daughter had a little accident, and we're so sorry."

"Julie Davenport?" asked Brian, his voice easing up. "As in, *the* Julie Davenport?"

"Yes, that's me," said Julie.

"Wow, I love your work."

Her mother laughed. "Well, you must have a very good memory."

"You're unforgettable. I can't believe we're actually talking. I heard that you lived in this neighborhood, but I didn't believe it." Brian's tone had changed completely. He sounded like he was talking to an old friend.

Allie hung up. Leave it to her mom to smooth things over. People just loved her. It was funny that her mom always talked about Mindy the model's spectacular quality, that undefinable, vague but definitely real thing. Because as far as Allie was concerned, her mother had it too. At parties, people gravitated toward Julie. When she told a story, everyone leaned closer to listen. At fancy restaurants, even the snootiest of hostesses were super sweet to her.

Cameron had some of it, too. At school, guys' eyes tracked Cameron's movements as she strutted down the hall. Everyone who wasn't Cameron's friend wanted to be.

And it wasn't just the students. Teachers, too, adored Cameron. She was bright and enthusiastic, an A student who was always the first to answer questions and do extra credit even when she didn't need it. When Allie's teachers recognized her last name, their eyes lit up. They were always so hopeful, expecting greatness until the first assignment was handed in.

Of course, all of this was unspoken. To acknowledge it would bring to the surface what she'd rather keep buried.

Allie headed back into Cameron's room so she could look at herself again. Cupping her hand around her nose, she tried to imagine it being small and straight. She and Cameron had the same eyes. Would Dr. Glass give her the same cute nose? Would that make her look like Cameron, and would she therefore be more like Cameron? And about that vague quality . . . was it something she had to learn? Or something that would just magically happen once she was pretty?

CHAPTER FIVE

Cameron felt like a complete and total fraud. "I really don't want to talk about it," she said, covering her face with her hands but still feeling four pairs of eyes watching her.

There was no getting out of this one. So Cameron told her friends the whole story, from her unfortunate nickname to the daily taunting: the name-calling, the tripping, the bra-cutting incident, and more. She told them how practically the whole school was involved, but that the major players were all sharing the beach house next door.

Lucy broke the shocked silence with a laugh that made Cameron bristle. At least until she realized it wasn't a mean laugh. "Oh, Cameron! They sound so horrible."

"You have no idea," Cameron mumbled.

"So what, you were going to change your name and pretend like those guys were strangers for the entire week?" asked Hadley.

"Oh my gosh. It's just like this novel I'm reading," said Ashlin. "*Flavor of the Month.* The main character is this plain-Jane actress who's super talented but can only do obscure, off-Broadway theater because she's not pretty enough. But then she comes into some money, and she decides to go to a plastic surgeon. She gets everything done: liposuction, tummy tuck, breast lift, nose job, chin and cheek implants—the works. It takes forever, but once she's done, she's gorgeous and she moves to LA and becomes a huge star."

"How so totally cheddar," Hadley said.

"Huh?" asked Ashlin.

"She means it's cheesy," Taylor explained.

"Well, I happen to like cheese," Ashlin replied. "Especially cheddar."

"I'm more of a manchego girl myself," said Lucy.

"You're blowing this way out of proportion," said Cameron. "All I did was have a nose job. And all I wanted to do today was prove to them that I'm different. You guys have no idea what they put me through. They were such assholes."

"Well, you did prove it," said Taylor. "That Hunter guy was so into you, Cam. At least he was until his girlfriend showed up."

"Were they *all* that mean?" asked Ashlin. "Even Devon?"

Cameron shrugged. Of course he was. She just didn't want to say so because obviously Ashlin liked him.

"All guys in junior high school are jerks," said Lucy. "It's a maturity issue. Know what they called me in the sixth grade? Large Lucy."

"Shut up," said Taylor.

"I'm serious. There were three Lucys in my class: Little Lucy, Regular Lucy, and Large Lucy. I went to fat camp."

"You did not," said Hadley.

As Lucy nodded, her soft green eyes grew larger. "For two summers in a row. But those camps don't really work, because you gain back all the weight, like two months after you're home. That's why my parents built an Olympic-size swimming pool at our house in LA. Know that charm bracelet hanging on my rearview mirror? My parents used to give me a charm for every pound I lost. They made me swim to lose weight, but I really loved it."

Cameron looked at her friends and realized that they could neither confirm nor deny the story, since Lucy had been a transfer student in eighth grade.

"I used to wear glasses," Ashlin blurted out. "Thick ones, too. But then I had LASIK surgery before I started high school."

"Right, I remember when we started freshman year," said Hadley. "I didn't even recognize you."

"Thanks a lot."

"No, I mean it as a compliment," said Hadley. "You stopped getting those perms, too, huh?"

"No, the frizz head is natural," said Ashlin. "I actually

started getting my hair straightened that summer."

"Wow," said Hadley. "Not that I should talk, since I had braces for three years."

"I only had them for two years," said Taylor. "It was still bad, though. And in eighth grade I tried to bleach my own hair, and it looked like I was wearing a stack of hay on my head."

"That's why you got that supershort haircut?" asked Ashlin.

Taylor nodded. "I had to."

"You guys don't understand," said Cameron. "I was *the* nerd, the one everyone avoided. Seriously. People averted their eyes when I walked down the hall."

"But who cares?" said Lucy. "Look at you now. You're so hot, those girls are jealous. And they should be."

"Totally," said Ashlin. "You should have seen their faces when they walked up and saw us talking to their guys."

"'Their guys.'" Lucy scoffed. "Like they own them."

"Which they don't," said Hadley. "Hunter totally wanted you."

"I know," said Ashlin. "There was so much sexual tension. It was palpable."

"So what was your nose like before?" asked Lucy.

"Horrible," said Cameron. "I don't want to think about it."

"Did the surgery hurt?" Taylor asked.

"No." Cameron shrugged. "I don't think so, anyway. It was

a while ago, so it's hard to remember. It was kind of freaky being under anesthesia, though. I was hooked up to an IV, and there were all these doctors and nurses around, and someone asked me to count to ten and I remember starting, but I guess I never made it to the end. The next thing I know, I'm waking up talking to myself. I don't remember what I said. I asked the anesthesiologist, but he pretended he didn't know."

"And that was it?" asked Lucy.

Cameron unconsciously scratched her nose. "No, I had packing in my nose for a while, so I had to breathe through my mouth, and my eyes were black and blue. Basically, I looked like I'd been beaten up. But they took out the packing a few days later, and the splint came off soon after that. It was still really red and swollen, but by the end of the summer I was completely normal-looking."

"I so want a nose job," said Hadley.

"Really?" Cameron considered her friend. Hadley was sitting on the couch, her tanned legs crossed. Her hair was naturally golden blond so she didn't have to stress over dark roots like Cameron and Taylor did. Plus, Hadley wasn't wearing any makeup, and she still looked beautiful. "Why?"

"Oh, don't pretend you don't know," said Hadley. She turned sideways so Cameron could see her profile, and pointed to the middle of her nose. "This bump is ridiculous."

Everyone looked. The bump was so small, Cameron hadn't

noticed it once in the three years the two had been friends. And that said a lot, since Cameron was hyperaware of other people's noses.

"They wouldn't even have to break the bone. All they'd have to do is pull back my skin and shave it down, but my parents said no," Hadley explained.

"I wouldn't worry about it," said Lucy.

"Seriously," said Taylor. "I never even think about it."

"Easy for you to say. You have a perfect nose," said Hadley.

Taylor beamed. "You think?"

Hadley nodded.

"Oh, but it doesn't matter, because my chin is so weak. My parents would be fine with me getting an implant, but only if I pay for it myself. And I don't have that kind of money."

There she goes again, thought Cameron. Just because Hadley wanted plastic surgery, Taylor had to invent some reason to want it too. All of Taylor's features were pretty great, so it must have been challenging to find something wrong with herself, but a weak chin? That was stretching it. Who got chin implants?

Not that Cameron could criticize, out loud, since she was the only one who'd actually had surgery. (LASIK was different. It didn't really count.)

"Wait, your parents are okay with it?" asked Lucy.

Taylor laughed. "They both get Botox injections, and my

mom had her eyes done last year. It would be hypocritical of them *not* to be okay with it."

"How much does a chin implant cost?" asked Ashlin.

"Around five thousand dollars, total," said Taylor. "That's including the surgery, the hospital fees, and the anesthesiologist's fee, and everything else."

"Wait, you know this?" asked Cameron.

Taylor nodded. "I should have that much saved up by the end of the summer, but if I blow it all on an implant, I'll be broke, and I really don't want to have to get a job at school."

"At least you can afford it if you really want it, though," said Hadley. "A nose job would cost eight thousand dollars. I asked my parents if they'd split the cost with me, but they freaked."

"Wait, how do you guys know?" asked Ashlin.

"We met with a surgeon a few months ago," said Hadley.

"You did?" asked Cameron.

Hadley and Taylor nodded. "We went together," Taylor explained.

"Why are you so surprised?" asked Lucy. "Didn't you do the same thing?"

Cameron shook her head. "Are you kidding? I was too young. My parents took care of everything. When I came home crying in junior high school, they told me they'd get my nose fixed when I was old enough, and then, a few days after my fifteenth birthday, they took me to the surgeon."

"You're so lucky," said Taylor.

"If I was really lucky, I'd have been born looking more like my mom," said Cameron, embarrassed to admit this out loud because it was so very true.

Julie Davenport hadn't worked in eighteen years, but people still recognized her and sometimes stopped her on the street. She was that striking. Cameron never understood why her mom had given it all up. She couldn't imagine having that kind of power and wasting it.

"Remember when I dated Leo from sophomore year and I went into his room and found an old pinup of your mom on his wall?" asked Hadley.

Everyone laughed except for Cameron, who shuddered. She was both creeped out and flattered by this. In a weird way, it also made her feel like a failure. No one would ever have a pinup of her on the wall. Cameron was pretty, but obviously she wasn't pretty enough.

"Anyway, you do look like her," said Lucy.

"Thanks," said Cameron, not really believing her friend.

When her mom was Cameron's age, she was living in a New York City loft with three other models, traveling between Milan and Tokyo like the two destinations were across town from each other. Julie always told her daughters that their lives were so much better, and that she had worked because she had to, because without the money or the grades for college, she'd had no other options. Modeling and acting,

Julie said, were only glamorous from the outside. Photo shoots were boring and stretched on for hours. Living that life meant being judged constantly. Having strangers look at you as if to say, *Are you pretty enough?* and *Are you something special?* every single day. It was the kind of pressure that could really mess with your head. In the end, Julie didn't want or need it.

Cameron believed her mom, and she preferred being on the other side of the camera anyway. Still, being the undiscovered daughter of someone who'd been discovered felt lousy. Deep down, Cameron felt like every day that she wasn't discovered, she was being judged. Judged as not being worthy.

Getting this power, this acceptance, so suddenly in the tenth grade merely made her hungry for more.

In Cameron's secret fantasy, she's having lunch at an outdoor café when she's approached by a famous director who begs, literally begs her to be in his next film. *Sorry,* she says, all blasé, as if this sort of thing happens to her all the time, *but my studies are more important. Thanks for asking, though.*

"I so wish I could have a new nose," Hadley said with a sigh.

"And I wish I could have lipo on my arms," Ashlin mused. "They're so fat."

"I'll go on a diet with you," Lucy offered. "I want to lose fifteen pounds before I get to school."

"You don't need to lose any weight," said Ashlin.

"I know, but I want to counteract the freshman fifteen," Lucy replied. "I'm like freaking out 'cause it'll be impossible to stay thin on dorm food."

"I'm stressed about that too," said Hadley, staring down at her legs, which were toothpick-skinny.

"I hate starch, and I hear it's all starchy food." Lucy turned on the TV. One of the best things about her house was that it had more than five hundred cable channels and a very comfy couch. Twenty minutes later, Cameron fell asleep to *Pretty in Pink*, which wasn't a big deal since she'd seen it at least twenty times.

Cameron woke up a couple of hours later to Lucy shaking her.

"What are you doing?" Cameron asked, pulling away. "Let go."

"There's a party at the beach," said Lucy. "Get up."

Cameron groaned. "I cannot deal with the La Jolla crowd right now."

"It's not just the La Jolla people," said Lucy. "There are tons of guys out there."

"Really?" Cameron glanced at her friend skeptically. She wouldn't put it past Lucy to lie just to get her way. It was something they all did from time to time.

Yet Lucy seemed sincere. "There's a bachelor party six houses down from here. They built a bonfire and they totally want to party with us. They were so psyched when I told them I had four friends back at the house. Especially after I assured them we were all eighteen."

The story did sound plausible.

Cameron decided to believe her. "Geez, Lucy. You find guys the way other people find change on the sidewalk."

"I know—it's one of my best talents," said Lucy, triumphant, as she stood up and ran for the stairs. "Siesta time is over!" she shouted before running up to share the good news.

An hour later, after another shower and makeup application and six wardrobe changes, Cameron walked to the bonfire with her friends, trying to ignore the sinking feeling in the pit of her stomach. Lucy hadn't lied. There *were* a bunch of new guys at the beach. Cute, older guys too, but the La Jolla crowd was also there. Cameron's friends ignored them out of loyalty, choosing instead to flirt with the bachelor-party crowd.

Nerves still raw over the unexpected (and unwanted) reunion, Cameron stayed off to the side, more comfortable observing for the moment.

When Hunter approached a few minutes later, her first instinct was to bolt, but Cameron held her ground. She tried seeing him as a stranger.

Hunter had changed into loud orange Hawaiian-print shorts. His thick dark hair grew out instead of down. He was cute, but Cameron worried that if she hooked up with him, his goatee would scratch her face.

Yet why was she even thinking about him like that, when she had a much cuter boyfriend back home?

"So you really surprised us back there," Hunter said, laughing but not in a mean way.

"Tell me about it." Cameron ran her fingers through her hair. "I didn't recognize any of you guys, at all. Honestly."

It was a feeble excuse and they both knew it. Luckily, Hunter let it slide. "You really have changed." He looked her up and down in a manner that could not be misinterpreted.

"It was just a nose job," Cameron snapped. "Will you chill?"

"Sorry." Hunter tried again, staring into her eyes. "I didn't mean to piss you off. I'm just amazed is all, because you're so different. So, like, cool and happy."

Cameron shrugged. She didn't want to be attracted to Hunter. It annoyed her that he was being so nice. As if now that she was presentable, all was supposed to be okay?

Like she could ever forget their seventh-grade class trip to the San Diego Zoo. As the class walked past the cages holding the long-beaked cranes, Hunter had grabbed her and yelled, "Look out! One escaped!"

"I know I was kind of cocky back in junior high," Hunter said, like he knew what she was thinking. "So, um, sorry if I was a jerk."

"You were a jerk. There are no 'ifs' about it."

"Please don't hold it against me."

"Oh, I don't care," said Cameron, wishing this were true. She was annoyed with Hunter, but still interested. And annoyed that she was still interested.

"So, where are you going to school?"

"UCSB."

"No way," said Hunter. "My brother goes there."

"Really?"

"Yup. I used to visit him all the time. You'll do okay there. They don't call UCSB the University of Santa Barbies for nothing."

"What?" asked Cameron.

"Don't tell me you've never heard that before."

Cameron shook her head, feeling bad, like she was missing out on the punch line of a well-known joke.

"UCSB is the land of Santa Barbies—because so many of the girls there look like Barbie dolls," Hunter explained.

"Oh. I didn't realize." As lame as this was, it made Cameron think. Was she cute enough to be considered a Barbie doll? And when Hunter said she'd do "okay," did he mean just all right, or well? It's not like she could ask him to clarify.

Just then she heard her name. Not her name, exactly, though. "BEAKFACE!" someone shouted too loudly and from too far away.

Cameron cringed as Nikki approached. "Sorry," she said, putting her arm around Cameron. "I meant to say, 'Hello,

Beekman.' I still can't believe it's really you. I totally thought of you last month because we were doing etymology in English class, and I found out that Cameron means 'crooked nose' in Scottish. How ironic is that?"

It was actually the opposite of ironic. Or at least it had been until a few years ago, but Cameron was too upset to point this out. She'd already known what the name Cameron meant in Gaelic, and she resented her parents for it, as if in choosing her name, they'd sealed her fate. "Um, do you want something?" she asked Nikki. "Because this isn't really the best time."

Nikki's boobs were spilling out of a too-tight white tank top. It was like she was offering them up to the world, wrapped in a red lacy bra that was so visible, it made her tank top completely irrelevant.

Cameron was about to make a joke to that effect, but when she turned to Hunter, she found that he wasn't even looking at her. Rather, his back was to her and he was talking to Nikki. Leering at her hungrily. Had he really blown her off for the cruelest girl she knew? Nikki was attractive in a skanky way. She only had one thing Cameron didn't. Well, two things, really: great boobs.

Looking around, Cameron noticed that the party had grown larger. It was as if all the nearby houses had been tipped to one side and shaken, spilling out the beautiful people. All the women dressed the same, in triangle bikini tops with short shorts, miniskirts, or tiny sarongs, as if they all hailed from a country where sleeves were illegal. Cameron felt like her head was about to explode.

Her biggest nightmare had come true. She'd been humiliated in front of a crowd that used to make a sport out of humiliating her. Then she'd come back for more, only to be blown off.

Heading toward the cooler, she realized something depressing. Perhaps she'd already peaked. She was eighteen. Her mom had been discovered at seventeen, while serving chocolate-dipped cones at the Dairy Queen in Wisconsin. A modeling-agency scout had spotted her and three weeks later she was on a plane to New York.

Last summer Cameron had waited tables at the Grill. It was a really big deal that they hired her, because all of their waitresses were so beautiful. The restaurant was around the corner from the William Morris Agency, which is why she'd applied. Executives from Warner Brothers and Universal and Paramount lunched there, and so did the talent agents. Cameron had expected to meet at least a few. The circumstances couldn't have been more ideal. She'd collected plenty of business cards from older men, too: lawyers, accountants, a dentist, some guy in advertising. Yet she failed to attract the right *type* of older man. No one from William Morris expressed interest. She didn't meet one studio executive—not even anyone from Fox Television. She'd waited tables there for two months, waiting for something to happen, but nothing did. It was humiliating. A disaster.

As Cameron opened up her beer, she noticed Taylor sitting cross-legged on a rock a few yards from the edge of the party.

"Are you meditating?" asked Cameron, sitting down next to her.

"No, I've been benched," Taylor replied. "And I guess you have too."

"Huh?"

"Face it, we can't compete." Taylor gestured toward the crowd.

Ashlin, Lucy, and Hadley were doing fine—this she didn't mind. But the fact that Nikki could hold her own in this crowd? It was beyond depressing. It was enraging.

Cameron gulped down her beer, then went to get another.

She wondered if this was it for her. Maybe she was destined to become the type of girl who would always have to get her own drinks.

The thought made her shudder, so she pushed it out of her mind.

As she reached for another drink, she heard laughter from across the beach. It was unmistakably Devon and he was making fun of her. She just knew it. Through the dark, Cameron squinted. Devon was kissing Ashlin, who was giggling. Humiliation pulsed through her body. Then, through the hazy drunken layers, it dawned on Cameron. Of course they weren't laughing at her. She was paranoid. Still, she *felt* like the butt of some joke, which was almost as bad.

A slow, sick feeling crept up on her, infecting her whole body like food poisoning. Cameron knew this sensation all too well. It was just like being back in La Jolla.

Of course, now it was worse because she knew the other side.

What was going to happen in September, at UC Santa Barbie? What if all the girls looked like Nikki? What if they all wore triangle bikini tops to class? How would Cameron compete? She was wearing her favorite skimpy outfit now, and no one even cared. Forget about her secret desire to be discovered. She couldn't even keep up.

Cameron left the party. Stumbling back to the house, she collapsed on the couch and turned on the TV. An old MTV *Spring Break* episode flashed on the screen. Girls in bikinis gyrated, their boobs spilling out all over the place. She flipped the channel and found a *Girls Gone Wild* infomercial. Human Barbie dolls were everywhere—on TV and right next door. There was no escaping. Even her closest friends had perfect bodies. Well, Hadley and Lucy did, anyway. Ashlin's arms were on the thick side, and Taylor's butt was a little flat, but they all had boobs. Everyone in the world did except Cameron, or at least that's how it seemed.

Turning off the TV, Cameron found her cell phone and

called Blake. He didn't pick up and the call went to his voice mail, so she hung up and dialed again . . . and again, and again, until he finally answered.

"Do you still love me?" she asked.

Blake groaned. "Cameron, it's two thirty in the morning. I was sleeping."

"Do you think I'm prettier than Nikki?" she asked, because in her drunken logic, Blake knew all about what had happened and wasn't upset that Cameron had been attracted to Hunter, but was insulted that Hunter had blown her off for another woman.

"Who's Nikki?"

"So you're saying that I'm not prettier."

"You're drunk."

"So what. You still haven't answered me."

"I have to be at work at seven a.m. Um, drink a lot of water, okay? And get some sleep."

"Wait!" said Cameron. But Blake had already hung up.

Fabulous. Even her boyfriend thought she was ugly. As Cameron lay on the couch, she felt her spirits sink lower and lower. She was trapped in psychological quicksand.

She looked down at her too-flat chest. Just two hours ago she'd thought her top was sexy. Now it looked like something a child would wear. An ugly child. People pretended there was no such thing, but Cameron knew this was a lie, because she'd been one.

Her new nose had changed her life, but obviously it could only take her so far.

Cameron's head ached. She got up to find some aspirin and a glass of water and noticed Ashlin's copy of *Flavor of the Month*. She was too drunk to see straight, and it was total trash, but still, something in that story of transformation appealed to her. It wasn't like Cameron was so unfamiliar with it. Picking it up, she flopped back down. She tried to read but passed out before she'd made it past the first page.

CHAPTER SIX

"The Japanese tea garden on our left was generously donated by Steven Spielberg," Nancy Shepard, the volunteer coordinator, explained. "And this small koi pond was built by the president of the Directors Guild. His parents are residents here."

The Motion Picture Home of Los Angeles was actually twenty miles north of the city, in an entirely different area code and with an entirely different landscape. Its rolling green hills were dotted with low buildings. All of them had white stucco walls and red tile roofs, like miniature houses. With its group dining hall, activities center, and weekly bingo game, the old-age home seemed to Allie like a camp for very old people.

It seemed like a pleasant enough place to be, and Allie was glad, since she'd be volunteering there every afternoon until her surgery. She'd always planned on getting her school-required community service hours out of the way before school started. When she realized she wouldn't be able to work at Coach McAdams's soccer clinic, her mom had found her this job instead. Compared to working at the camp, it sounded kind of dull, yet Allie's mom had raved about the Motion Picture Home. It was very exclusive for a retirement community, only open to people who'd worked in the film industry. Her mom cared about that sort of thing. "Maybe your father and I will end up there someday," she'd joked.

Allie and the other two volunteers, Jenna and Bebe, practically had to jog to keep up with the brisk and efficient volunteer coordinator. As Nancy walked, her long dark braid swung back and forth across her back like the pendulum of a very precise clock.

"The bungalows are essentially self-contained one-bedroom apartments," she explained, "while the villas are more like hotel suites. Most of your time will be spent in the recreation center, playing games with the residents and reading to those who are blind. You'll also be delivering meals to the ones who can't leave their beds. Tonight you can wheel some of the residents from the dining hall to the screening room."

"Screening room?" asked Allie.

"We show movies here every night," Nancy explained as she handed each volunteer a clipboard with a list of names. "Tonight is *Gone with the Wind*. Allie, I need to warn you about Al. He's the third resident on your list. Please be careful, because he's a little fresh for a ninety-two-year-old."

"They're done with dinner now?" asked Allie, glancing at her watch.

Nancy nodded. "Yes. Please follow me."

"Didn't you know? Getting old means finishing dinner at five," Bebe whispered.

The three volunteers giggled.

"Something funny?" Nancy asked, turning around and looking at them with raised eyebrows.

"Nothing," Jenna said, quickly.

Once in the dining room, Nancy introduced Allie to her first "customer."

"Bernie Stevenson, please meet Allie Beekman, one of our new volunteers. Allie will be taking you to the movie. Will you show her where to go?"

Bernie's head was wrinkled and bald on top, with tufts of white hair that sprang from the sides and from his ears like cotton. The liver spots on his hands reminded Allie of muddy raindrops. "I worked on *Gone with the Wind*," he said cheerfully, as if this were a new way of saying hello.

"Really?" Allie wheeled him past the rose garden and over a wooden footbridge.

"Yes, I was the assistant director at the time, but I went on to direct many, many films. Classics." He rattled off a list of movies that Allie hadn't heard of, but she nodded anyway to be polite. She was glad he was so chatty, because usually old people made her feel flustered. She didn't know how to talk to them. All her grandparents had died years ago, so she didn't have any practice.

As she wheeled Bernie into the theater, he waved to a thin man wearing a plaid shirt and a tan beret. "I'll sit by Stan, over there," he said.

"Okay, here you go, Bernie," Allie said, carefully putting on the brake the way Nancy had demonstrated.

"Thank you, Jenny."

"My name is Allie."

He tilted his head to one side and blinked at her with murky blue eyes. "You look like a Jenny."

"Well, I'm not."

"Can I call you Jen, for short?"

"Um, sure," said Allie. "I'll see you later."

Allie hurried back to the dining hall to pick up a woman named Muriel von Deisel, who wore a crisp white pants suit, a platinum blond wig, and heavy bracelets that looked like gold handcuffs.

"What are they showing tonight?" she asked.

"*Gone with the Wind*," said Allie.

Muriel frowned down at her bracelets. "I've seen that one."

"Do you not want to go?" Allie looked around, not sure if this was actually an option.

"Of course I want to go. Why wouldn't I?"

"I don't know." Allie pushed the chair forward.

"Watch it. You're speeding." Muriel spoke sharply.

Allie slowed down, which wasn't easy, since they were moving downhill. She hadn't realized that wheelchairs were so heavy.

"I have a granddaughter who's about your age."

"Really?" asked Allie.

"She never visits," Muriel replied.

Allie's next customer was Al, and he didn't seem like a pervert at all. At least not at first. The poor old guy dropped his pen on the floor as soon as Allie introduced herself. Allie picked it up and handed it to him, but then he dropped it again. This went on and on, until she realized he was dropping it on purpose so he could watch her bend over.

"Cut it out," Allie said, not knowing whether to scold him or to laugh.

Al shrugged. "Sorry, but I've gotta entertain myself somehow."

Allie managed to get everyone else into the screening room without incident. When she was finished, she found Nancy clearing tables and directing some of the waitstaff in the nearly empty dining hall.

"I'm all done here," she said, handing in her clipboard.

"Thank you, Allie," said Nancy. "Can you do me a favor and go pick up one more resident? Her name is Eve and she lives in bungalow seventeen. It's the large one, surrounded by sunflowers."

"Okay."

"It's not going to be easy," Nancy warned her. "But don't take no for an answer."

Allie hadn't noticed bungalow seventeen before, which was strange since it was surrounded by a well-tended garden. Besides the giant sunflowers, there were African violets in the window boxes and small palm trees lining the cobblestone walkway. Allie knocked, but there was no answer. She peeked into the window by the door and saw the outline of a person sitting in the dark, faintly illuminated by a small desk lamp. She knocked again, calling, "Hello?"

"Nobody's home," the woman inside yelled.

Allie laughed and knocked again. "Um, I'm here to take you to the movie."

"I said no one's here." Her voice was deep and scratchy-sounding, like she had a sore throat.

"That's kind of hard to believe. Mind if I come in?"

"Well, I'm in no condition to stop you if I wanted to," the woman replied. "And for the record, I do want to stop you."

Allie opened the door. Eve's bungalow was larger than the others and it was also messier. An overflowing bookshelf lined one wall. The others were covered with oil paintings. Allie had never been to Europe, but she imagined that it looked a lot like the pictures on Eve's walls. The back ones showed the countryside: pale blue skies, fields of red and yellow tulips growing on low rolling hills. The wall opposite showed urban scenes: crowded cafés and rows of apartment buildings on cobblestone streets, with colorful laundry strung between windows.

From what Allie had seen during her tour, she knew that the other residents' rooms were decorated fairly sparsely. Most looked like they were occupied by people who had either just moved in or were planning on leaving soon. She'd seen plenty of family photos and old movie posters, and even a bunch of faded black-and-white headshots, but nothing else of this scope and scale.

"It's so beautiful in here," said Allie.

Eve closed her book, pushed it away from her, and took off her wire-rimmed bifocals. Her skin was like a pale, wrinkled bedsheet, and her eyes were deep blue and angry-looking.

"What are you doing here?" she asked sharply.

"Nancy sent me to take you to the movie. It's *Gone with the Wind*."

"I can't go."

"Nancy really wants you to," said Allie. "Um, do you need help getting into your wheelchair? Because I can call for an attendant."

"I am perfectly capable of getting into my own chair. The only reason I'm forced to use that thing is because the home is afraid of being sued." Eve stood up very slowly and walked across the room, easing herself into the wheelchair that was in the corner by the door. "And who are you?" she asked, peering up at Allie.

"Allie Beekman."

"How old are you, Allie Beekman?"

"Fifteen."

"Please use a complete sentence when you answer me."

Allie wheeled Eve outside and carefully closed the bungalow door. "Okay. I mean, um, okay, I will."

"Are you one of those volunteers from a high school that has a community-service requirement?" asked Eve, as Allie pushed her along. "Or are you here because you want to be?"

Well, she wasn't as friendly as most of the residents, but she sure was sharp.

"Can't the answer to both of those questions be yes?" Allie asked.

"Oh, I highly doubt it," said Eve. "This is your first day here, I take it?"

"It's that obvious, huh?"

"What's obvious is that 'huh' is not a word. So tell me, Allie, what do you think of the place?"

"It's nice. I like it."

Eve grunted. "Too many old people here for my tastes. I like to think of these lawns as grazing land. Essentially, we're all cows that have been put out to pasture."

"That's so cynical," said Allie. "This is a beautiful, peaceful place."

"Like a sanitorium."

Allie was beginning to understand why Nancy had warned

her about Eve. She'd almost rather deal with Al the pervert. At least he was nice.

Just then her cell phone sang from her pocket. Pulling it out, she checked the caller ID. It was Quincy, her best friend.

Eve raised her voice to a throaty chirp. "In my day people knew better than to answer the phone while they were in the middle of a conversation."

"Sorry." Allie turned off her phone without answering it. Then she tucked it back into her pocket.

As she headed past the koi pond, she heard someone call her name. Surprised, Allie turned around.

"Over here," said Julie, waving.

"Hi, Mom," Allie called.

As Julie walked closer, she said, "I was going to wait in the parking lot, but I've always wanted to see what this place looked like, so I thought I'd take a walk around."

"I'm almost ready. I just have to drop Eve off at—"

"Do not talk about me as if I am a piece of luggage," Eve said, interrupting.

"Sorry, Eve. Please meet my mother, Julie Davenport. Mom, this is Eve. You never told me your last name."

"Santora," Eve replied.

"Eve Santora," Julie repeated, her eyes widening. "You're Eve Santora. I can't believe it. It's such an honor to meet you. I'm a huge fan." She crouched down and grasped Eve's hand.

Eve nodded and smiled, ever so slightly. Perhaps it was Allie's imagination, but she seemed to sit up straighter.

"Allie, honey, do you know who this is?" Julie took off her sunglasses as if she needed to get an unobstructed view to confirm it. "Eve Santora is a legend," she announced.

"I'm not dead yet," Eve said.

Allie laughed, but her mom was mortified.

"I'm sorry. I didn't mean that," Julie said in a clumsy attempt to backpedal. "I'm a big fan of your work. I used to act also. I mean, I still do. And when I started out, I watched all of your movies, again and again."

"I'm going to miss tonight's film," said Eve, looking up at Allie. "We'd better go."

"Right," said Allie. "I'll be right back, Mom."

"It was lovely meeting you," Julie called, waving somewhat frantically.

After Allie delivered Eve to the screening room, she headed for the parking lot, where her mom was waiting in the rented car. (Her own car was still in the shop, which Allie felt very bad about.)

"I can't believe you get to spend time with Eve Santora," said Julie. "This is such an amazing opportunity for you."

Allie rolled her eyes. "It's not like we're hanging out. I was only dropping her off at the movie."

"I didn't even know she was still alive. Eve was so beautiful, Allie. Even through the wrinkles you can tell, can't you?"

"I guess," said Allie, who actually hadn't given the matter much thought.

"Don't tell me you've never heard of her."

Allie shook her head.

"Oh, Allie. She was the biggest movie star of her day. You've heard of Katharine Hepburn and Grace Kelly and Marilyn Monroe?"

"Um, sure."

"Well, Eve was more glamorous than them all. She was only in half a dozen films, and for some reason she just disappeared. I have all of her old movies at home. We should watch them."

Allie agreed. She had to, or her mom would be disappointed. Of course, Allie was also curious.

A few hours later Allie and her mom watched the final credits of *An Oriental Sunrise*, Eve's first starring role. Allie had to admit that her mother was right. Eve was an amazing performer. It was hard to believe that the beautiful actress she'd just watched on TV and the crabby old woman she'd met at the Motion Picture Home were the same person. It didn't seem possible.

They were about halfway through Eve's second movie when the phone rang. Julie picked it up and a few moments later handed it over to Allie. "It's Quincy," she said.

"Hey," Allie said.

"Where have you been? I left you three messages on your cell."

"Sorry," said Allie. "I had to turn it off during my community service and I guess I forgot about it."

"I've been dying to talk to you. You'll never guess what Larkin is doing next week."

"What?" asked Allie.

"It's crazy. I want you to guess first."

"I hate guessing. Just tell me."

"She's getting a nose job."

Allie felt sick to her stomach. She hadn't told any of her friends about her own plans for surgery. She was kind of hoping that it would just happen and they wouldn't notice. It was stupid, but so much easier than actually talking about it.

"Hello?" asked Quincy. "Are you still there?"

"How do you know?"

"I called her to see if she still wanted to bunk with us in Colorado—I'm helping Coach McAdams with the list—and she told me she wasn't going to play next year. I was like, 'Why?' And she just admitted it. The team will be fine—she wasn't even that good—but still. She's going to do yoga instead. Can you believe it?"

Yoga was what the pretty girls did instead of gym. Allie's sister had actually campaigned to get the program on campus two years before.

"Wow," said Allie.

"I know," said Quincy. "It's the craziest thing, right?"

Allie didn't say anything. She couldn't even bring herself to agree.

"Um, are you okay?" asked Quincy.

"Sure," Allie replied weakly. "You're right. That's really crazy."

CHAPTER SEVEN

Cameron had prepared more thoroughly for this moment than she had for the SATs, which she'd aced. The five days she'd been back from Cabo had been spent doing copious amounts of research. She'd met with doctors, had spent countless hours online, and knew all of the statistics. Her plan was flawless. There was nothing her parents could say that would make her change her mind. No argument she couldn't counter. So, she wondered, why was she still so nervous?

It was 9:00 a.m. on Saturday and her parents were sitting at the kitchen table, waiting for her the way she'd asked. She'd specifically scheduled this meeting when she knew that Allie would be out of the house. She wasn't sure why, exactly, but she didn't want her little sister to overhear this. Quite honestly, she wished she could take care of the whole thing without Allie ever knowing, but that was something that not even she would be able to swing.

Cameron opened up her notebook and passed her parents each a piece of paper.

"What's this?" asked her father, Jeffrey. As usual, he'd been up since six o'clock and had already run five miles and read three newspapers. It was intimidating on a normal day, but today even more so, because Cameron knew that the news she was about to deliver would make him uncomfortable and perhaps even angry.

"It's an outline," said Cameron. "Of the points I want to make. I want you to know that I've given this a lot of thought. This isn't something I'm jumping into. I've spoken to many people about it."

"About what?" asked Julie.

"You'll see." Cameron consulted her own copy of the outline, feeling silly for treating her parents as if they were in a company board meeting. But this was how she got what she wanted in her family. At sixteen she'd impressed her father with auto-safety statistics enough to convince him to buy her an Audi (used but still really cool). And this past spring she'd listed the advantages of going to a public, UC school versus a private college back east when she'd informed them of her decision not to go to Penn, her dad's alma mater. This current issue was a lot more personal and not the kind of thing she wanted to discuss in front of her dad, but she knew there was no other way. She had to get through it. This was too important. In the end, it would be worth the discomfort.

Cameron cleared her throat and read. "My first point is this: I morph my body in many ways. In fact, I've been doing so since I was nine when I got my ears pierced. Mom, you and I diet together sometimes. I go to yoga three times a week, which builds muscle. Pilates and sit-ups have changed the definition in my abs. I wore braces for two and a half years to shift my teeth into place. All of these practices have had a physical impact on my body. A change of my actual flesh, if you will. What I'm asking for now is no different."

Frowning, Jeffrey scanned the outline. "What are you asking for? You don't say."

Ignoring him, Cameron read on. "Two: My image, the way I present myself to the world, is constantly in flux. I wear makeup. I get my hair highlighted and cut every other month. I got spray-on tan before the prom, and even regular tanning is something that changes my body. One day at the beach and my image has changed, ever so slightly, right? Also, I pluck my eyebrows, and I get bikini waxes. All stuff you both approve of. Some of it you even pay for."

"And some of it I don't need to be reminded about," Jeffrey said with a groan.

"Sorry, Dad, but this is important to my larger point."

"Cameron, what are you getting at? Please just tell us where you're going with this, or we're going to think the worst," said Julie.

Cameron started to worry, knowing the "worst" her mom

spoke of was probably exactly what she was about to reveal. But she had to get through this. Her parents were her only obstacle, and they'd never been able to stop her from getting what she wanted before. "Just bear with me," she said. "Now, three: You've already sanctioned cosmetic surgery in the past; as we all know, my nose job three years ago was your idea, Mom. You made the appointment for me just like you did for Allie. So this is not really any different."

"What's not any different?" asked her mother.

"Patience," said Cameron. "I'm getting there. My fourth point: It's not like I want anything unnatural or trendy, like a tattoo. This is not something I'll regret in five years. This is something that's important to me. I've given this a lot of thought and I know what I'm getting into. I understand the risks and the dangers involved. What I want is to correct something about my body that I've been self-conscious about for years. It will be perfectly natural-looking, and it really isn't a big deal when you think about it logically . . ."

Cameron sneaked a peek at her parents. They were looking at each other nervously. Taking a deep breath, she continued. "According to the American Society for Aesthetic Plastic Surgery, in 2005 there were eleven-point-five million cosmetic procedures performed in this country. What I plan to do is the second most common medical one. There were 364,610 of them performed last year. Rounding up, that's half a million."

"That's actually very far from half a million," Jeffrey observed.

"Where are you going with all this?" asked her mom.

Cameron swallowed hard. This was it. Her points had seemed legitimate when she was coming up with them and putting them down, all neat and clear, on the brand-new laptop they'd given her for college. So why was she having such a hard time now? Why did her argument feel so flimsy?

"Promise you won't freak out?" Cameron cursed herself for asking. She didn't need their permission, she reminded herself. That's not what this was about. She was an adult now. She could vote, go to prison, drink alcohol in most countries . . .

"Just tell us what you want," Jeffrey said, in a stern tone of voice that Cameron wasn't used to.

Taking a deep breath, Cameron looked her mother in the eye because she couldn't bear to look at her father. "I've been self-conscious about my flat chest for a long time, so I've finally decided to do something about it. I'm going to get breast implants."

Her mother gasped and brought her hand to her mouth in horror.

"No!" her father said, standing up so fast that the kitchen chair tipped over and crashed to the floor.

"Honey, you don't need this," said her mom. "This is crazy. You have a beautiful body. Your breasts included."

"You got into an Ivy League college," said her dad. "Why are you acting so stupid?"

"What's stupid about wanting to improve my body?" Cameron demanded.

Rather than answer her, Jeffrey turned to his wife. "I knew we should have forced her to go to Penn. If she was going to school back east, she wouldn't care about this kind of thing."

"UCSB is an excellent school," Cameron insisted.

"Did Blake put you up to this?" asked Julie.

"Blake?" Cameron said, amazed that her mom would ask such a thing. "Blake doesn't even know about this. This was my idea completely, and it's my decision. I'm an adult and this is what I want. This is what I'm doing."

"You are not," Jeffrey whispered urgently. "You can't."

Cameron was intimidated but unwilling to back down. "I have the money," she said.

"How do you have the money?" asked her mom.

"From babysitting and from waiting tables last summer."

"That's supposed to be your spending money for college," said her father.

Cameron shrugged. "So I'll get a job in the fall."

Jeffrey shook his head. "We agreed that you weren't going to get a job so you could focus on your studies. Do you know how competitive graduate schools are these days?"

"Dad, I'm not even thinking about graduate school yet. I

haven't even started college. Anyway, you can't tell me what to do with my money."

"Your money? How'd you like to put yourself through college?" her dad asked angrily. "Your money won't take you that far, Cameron."

"You wouldn't do that," said Cameron. "It's not fair to threaten me. I'm trying to be reasonable."

Her dad opened his mouth, but no words came. Strange, since Jeffrey never had a problem saying exactly what he wanted to. He turned to Julie, as if prompting her to speak, but she couldn't either. Finally, he left the room, shaking his head in disbelief as he headed upstairs.

Cameron sat down across from her mom. "I'm doing this," she said. "You can't stop me, because I'm not asking for your permission, and I wish you guys wouldn't make such a big deal out of this. It's a small thing, when you think about it. I have this problem, so I'm fixing it. End of story."

Tears streamed down Julie's face as she looked down at Cameron's outline. "Then why did you go to all this trouble? You obviously want something from us, and I hope it's not our approval, because you're not going to get that."

"Actually," said Cameron, "I only have four thousand dollars, which means I can afford to get implants from this guy in North Hollywood named Dr. Platt. He seems pretty young, so I guess that's why he's so cheap. I'd much rather go to Dr. Glass. Everyone says he does really great work, and look what he did to my nose. He has an opening, too, but his surgery would cost ten thousand dollars."

"You're asking us to *pay* for this?"

"I'm having the surgery either way. I thought that you'd want to help make sure it's safer, that I'm going to someone we all trust. If you give me the rest of the money, I promise to pay you back."

"Jeffrey!" Julie walked to the doorway and called out, "Jeffrey, come down here, now!"

"I can't face Dad. He's too angry."

"Then go to your room."

"You can't ground me."

"Cameron, just go," said her mom.

And Cameron went.

A couple of hours passed before her parents came to speak with her. Well, at first only her mom did the talking. Her dad was too upset to utter a sound. His anger was so intense, it scared her.

"I'm trying to understand why you want this," said Julie.

"Because my chest is too flat. We've been through this already," said Cameron.

"We don't approve of your plans, and we'd like for you to reconsider," Julie said.

Cameron shook her head. "I've made up my mind. Dad, you're the one who's always telling me that if something bothers me, then rather than complain, I should find a way to make it better. Well, this is something that bothers me, so I'm fixing it."

Her father looked down at his feet. Clearly, this wasn't what he had in mind.

It was her mother who answered. "We listened to your presentation and now it's our turn to speak."

"Fine." Cameron crossed her arms over her chest and leaned back against her headboard.

"We don't condone what you're doing, but we're not going to let you go to an inexperienced doctor. Frankly, we're horrified that you're willing to do that to your body. So we will supplement your surgery, but only if you do some research on the risks involved."

"I've already done that," said Cameron. "Trust me."

"We would like a list of all of the risks, in outline form like the one you gave us this morning. But that's not all," said her mom. "We'll only give you spending money for college if you maintain a 3.5 GPA."

"But that's not fair."

"You're right," said Julie. "It's more than fair. It's generous. And we know you're capable."

"Okay, fine. Is that all?" asked Cameron.

Julie cringed. "You don't want to be too big, do you?"

"No, not at all," said Cameron. "Don't worry. I just want to be a C cup, like you."

Cameron's parents looked at each other but didn't say anything.

"What?" asked Cameron.

"Nothing," said her mom, and they filed out of her room.

Lying down on her bed, Cameron stared at the ceiling. Things hadn't gone well, but they had gone, and once more Cameron had gotten what she wanted.

For once, though, getting what she wanted actually felt pretty lousy. Perhaps it had something to do with the fact that during the whole conversation, her father hadn't said a word.

Worse than that, he couldn't even bring himself to look at her.

CHAPTER EIGHT

The two-mile trip to the top of the canyon at Griffith Park was steep and offered no shade, but Quincy sprinted up as if she were being chased by an evil green monster.

Allie pumped her arms as hard as she could and willed her legs to move faster. They'd been doing this run every morning for a week now. It wasn't a race. They ran together for fun, yet both were acutely aware of the fact that Quincy always finished first. What irritated Allie was that each time she made it look so effortless.

"So I just talked to Larkin again, and she's freaking out about her nose job," said Quincy, who'd hardly broken a sweat.

"Huh," Allie replied noncommittally. Plastic surgery was the last thing she wanted to talk about. She'd managed to change the subject every time Quincy brought it up. And it seemed as if Quincy brought it up constantly. Allie was sick of it.

She was also running too hard to carry on a conversation. At the moment, she only cared about beating Quincy. With all this talk about Larkin's surgery, not to mention the whole varsity soccer issue, getting to the top first had taken on more significance.

Allie ran as fast as she could, but by the third switchback they were still shoulder to shoulder.

"I don't blame her for being scared. The whole anesthesia thing is risky. And what if Dr. Hsu messes up? There's no going back."

Allie didn't answer.

Dr. Hsu was a well-known plastic surgeon, and their friend Carly's father. It wasn't crazy that Quincy was talking about this, but Allie's paranoia still kicked in. Could Quincy somehow know about her appointment with Dr. Glass? Was she talking about this because she wanted Allie to admit she was getting a nose job?

"Still, I can't wait to see what she looks like afterward."

Maybe the idea had Quincy so intrigued because no one would ever think she needed plastic surgery herself. Quincy had long blond hair, blue eyes, a cute nose that turned up like a ski jump, and crazy high cheekbones. She used to be skinny with knobby knees and braces, but now she was thin and beautiful by any standard. Allie knew because Cameron had told her so. She said it as if she were complimenting Allie. Like, *Good for you for sticking it out through her awkward years, because now your best friend is hot, and that definitely reflects well on you.*

As if prettiness were a virtue that translated into coolness—like it could be measured, and having a pretty best friend meant bonus points. Like Allie needed all the help she could get.

Basically, her sister and her best friend were the same type of girl.

And the proof? A few weeks ago the three of them were shopping at the Beverly Center, and some sales guy at Sunglass Hut assumed that Quincy and Cameron were sisters. When Cameron corrected his mistake and explained that Allie was her sister, the guy didn't believe her. He seemed to think they were all playing some joke on him.

By getting plastic surgery, Allie would end up looking more like her very own sister. Did that mean she'd look more like Quincy, too? If she dyed her hair blond, would people mistake them for sisters? And was this what she was supposed to strive for?

Quincy picked up the pace, kicking up dirt as she ran. When she pulled ahead, Allie leaned forward. They weren't racing, but Allie was *not* going to let her win.

Of course, whenever she managed to catch up, Quincy ran harder, until both of them were sprinting.

The pace was excruciating, and soon Quincy pulled farther ahead. Her blond ponytail bobbed as her feet pounded the ground.

They were both red-faced, but only Allie was sweating. They had almost reached the top. Allie had to beat her, just this once. Allie imagined Dr. Glass chasing her, with his scalpel in hand. She started laughing so hard she almost tripped, but it did the trick. In a sudden burst of energy she made it to the top first. She finished less than a second faster than Quincy but still before her, and they both knew it.

"Nice," said Quincy. She pretended that she didn't mind losing, but Allie could tell that she did.

Of course, she could only take pleasure in this victory for a few seconds. Soon Allie cramped up so badly, she cowered over. She stretched her aching thighs, even though the act of stretching brought more pain.

At least Quincy pretended not to notice her suffering. "So with Larkin out, who do you want in our cabin?"

"Doesn't matter." Allie waited for Quincy to mention the one spot on the varsity team, but she didn't. Whether that was because she didn't know about it or because she was pretending not to, Allie couldn't tell.

CHAPTER NINE

"Congratulations," Blake whispered in Cameron's ear. "You have officially survived your first night in the desert."

Cameron opened her eyes. The sun was shining through the walls of the tent, casting everything in a bluish tint. It was hot and musty-smelling, and sand had gotten everywhere: in the corners of the tent, under her sleeping bag, on her pillow, and in her hair. But there were no cockroaches, ants, or other insects, and for that she was grateful.

One night down and one to go, she thought as she rolled over and faced Blake. She'd only agreed to go camping in the first place because she knew how much it would mean to him. She loved him dearly, from his thick, sandy blond hair that refused to part evenly all the way down to the woven hemp bracelet wrapped around his tanned ankle.

They'd been together for almost a year, Cameron's longest relationship ever. Though Blake was undeniably hot, he existed outside of Bel Air Prep's regular social hierarchy. He didn't play soccer or any other sport, and he ate lunch with the granola crowd: girls who refused to shave their legs and preached feminism, guys who slouched and ranted about their awesome bass guitars. Sometimes he wore a beret, and he'd never even been to a cool party until Cameron started dating him.

Yet all of that was part of his attraction. Cameron had gone out with plenty of popular guys at Bel Air Prep, but she could never trust them. Whenever a new one flirted with her, her first thought was always, *He's kidding. This isn't real.* A holdover from her Beakface days.

Blake was different, and Cameron had sought him out because of it. She assumed her friends wondered about her choice, but no one had ever questioned it. Probably because Blake was so hot.

Dating him was easy. Well, except for the whole camping thing. Civilization had progressed. There was no need to sleep in tents.

"I've been to the desert before," she said as she sat up and smoothed down her hair, happy that there was no mirror around because she knew she must look truly frightening.

Blake laughed. "Las Vegas doesn't count." He climbed out of his sleeping bag and started digging around in his giant red backpack. Cameron couldn't believe the stuff he'd already pulled out of there: the tent, two sleeping bags and air mattresses, all his clothes, their food, a camping stove, and half their water.

Cameron played up her discomfort, purely for the entertainment value. "Seriously. It was really rustic. The Bellagio lost our reservation, and there were like a hundred conventions in town, so we couldn't find a decent place to stay. We ended up at this nasty Motel Six two miles from the Strip. Can you imagine?"

Apparently, Blake wasn't in the mood. There was no trace of humor in his voice when he said, "Come on, Cam. It's total sacrilege comparing a Motel Six to Joshua Tree National Park." He pushed aside the giant pack and started going through his day pack.

"I was just kidding," she said, annoyed that she had to point this out. "What are you looking for, anyway?"

"My toothbrush. Aha!" He pulled out his dop kit and smiled triumphantly. "Be back in a minute."

"Wait for me." Cameron had been dying to pee for an hour but was too scared to leave the tent by herself in the dark. Apparently, snakes were more active at the park during the summer, but by the time Blake had warned her of this, it was too late to turn around and go home.

"My back is killing me," she said as she climbed out of the tent and stretched.

"You rolled off your air mattress in the middle of the night. I tried to tell you, but you wouldn't wake up."

Cameron was momentarily freaked that Blake had seen her sleeping. What if she'd been drooling or something? Sometimes she talked in her sleep. What if she'd said something ridiculous?

"What's wrong?" asked Blake.

"Nothing," she replied.

"Don't you love sleeping out in the wilderness?"

Their campsite was nestled between two large boulders, a five-minute walk to the bathroom area. Which was good, because they couldn't see or hear anyone else, but also bad for that same reason.

"Honestly? I've seen too many bad horror movies to enjoy it," said Cameron. "I was up half the night worried there was some guy with a hook for a hand lurking nearby, just waiting to sneak into our tent and maul us. This is the classic scenario, and as a pretty blonde, I'm a walking target."

"So that's why you made me sleep by the opening?"

Cameron nodded. "It's still not safe, though. Any psycho with a nail clipper could rip right through this flimsy thing. Probably with a pair of tweezers, even."

"You're too much." Blake grabbed Cameron around the waist, picked her up and spun her around.

"Look out. I have morning breath." She pulled her face away and covered her mouth with one hand when Blake tried to kiss her.

"I don't care," Blake said, but he put her back down anyway.

Cameron took a few steps away and looked around. "Now which way is the bathroom?"

"You're too much." Blake laughed, thinking she was pulling some fake "ditzy blonde lost in the wilderness" routine. Good thing he didn't realize she was serious.

After they washed up and got dressed and ate some lumpy oatmeal, they set out for a hike. Blake was sweet enough to carry all their water, leaving Cameron with her camera and their lunch, neither of which weighed much.

"You'll get great shots on this trail," said Blake.

"I can't wait," said Cameron, meaning, *I can't wait until this hike is over and the sun goes down so we can go to sleep and wake up and pack and finally leave this place.*

Still, as much as she was looking forward to being back in LA, she had to admit that Joshua Tree was stunning. It was covered in funky red-orange rock formations, with patches of purple wildflowers scattered about and the coolest-looking cactus-type trees she'd ever seen. After an hour of walking, she hardly minded the heat, or the way it made her sweat like a pig in a wool blanket. She just wished they were staying at a hotel instead. Or at the very least at a campsite that had hot-water showers and someplace to plug in her hair dryer.

That was the price she had to pay in order to go out with a granola. Next time, she decided, she'd find a guy with a deeper appreciation for indoor plumbing. And even though it seemed wrong to think about her next boyfriend when she was on vacation with her current one, Cameron couldn't help herself. It was just who she was. Whenever she heard her favorite song on the radio, she still felt compelled to change the station, always in search of something better.

After scrambling up a particularly steep hill, Blake stopped and took off his T-shirt. Then he pulled out a bottle of water. "You okay?" he asked.

"Great." Cameron was out of breath, but happy at least to be getting such a great workout.

He offered her the water. "Want some?"

"No, you go first." After pushing her sweaty bangs from her face, she took off her lens cap and pointed the camera toward Blake. When he tipped his head back to drink, she snapped a few shots.

"The scenery is much more interesting than I am," he said, wiping his mouth with the back of his hand.

"I'll be the judge of that." Cameron wanted to get a good shot of him to enlarge for her dorm room wall. (Even though she thought about moving on, she still wanted proof that she'd once dated a guy with perfect biceps and a washboard stomach.)

"Here." As he tried to hand her the bottle, she continued to snap away.

He shielded his eyes from the sun. "Come on. That's enough."

"You look amazing, Blake. Seriously. You're like a model, advertising Nalgene bottles or tourism in California or something."

"Yeah, that's me." Blake rolled his eyes. "You know, Joshua trees don't grow anywhere else in the world. I thought you'd want to shoot them."

Cameron paused to wipe a speck of dust from her lens. "There are plenty in the background."

"Don't you want pictures of the landscape without me in the way?"

Lowering her camera, she leaned against a large rock on the side of the trail. "Nature shots don't really fit into the theme of my work."

"What theme?"

"Well," said Cameron, "I'm just more into taking pictures of beautiful people rather than beautiful scenery."

"Isn't that kind of, I don't know . . ." Blake's voice trailed off, but Cameron knew exactly what he meant: "superficial." They'd had arguments like this before, and it drove her crazy. Just because she liked to shop and would rather watch *Legally Blonde* than, say, *Being John Malkovich* didn't make her shallow. It only made her honest.

"I just think that people are a much more worthy subject matter than inanimate objects. Even ones as stunning as this. Plus, think about it. Every single tourist who comes to this park takes tons of pictures of the Joshua trees and the wildflowers and the desert landscape. So what's unique about that? Anyone can capture something beautiful that exists in nature, but making people look beautiful? That's the sort of thing David Champlain is into. He's built a whole career based on it."

"Beautiful by whose definition?" Blake asked.

"Society's," said Cameron, with a shrug. It annoyed her when he acted virtuous like this. "Don't pretend like you don't know what I mean."

"Can't you do some of both?" asked Blake. "I mean, look at where we are."

"I don't think the park's true nature can be captured on film, anyway. It's in the air and the smell and in the general feeling of this place, right?"

"Ansel Adams did an amazing job of capturing Yosemite," said Blake.

"Perhaps, but Ansel Adams isn't teaching a one-time workshop at UCSB." She didn't mean to sound cold. It was just her "eye on the prize" mentality talking. "Anyway, Ansel Adams focused on beauty in the natural world, so he got great pictures without even trying. My approach to photography is the opposite. I really love that a picture can lie. That you can take a regular person and make that person seem spectacular."

"Suit yourself." Blake shrugged. "I thought you weren't sending your portfolio in until the end of the summer."

"I'm not, but my mom has this old friend who's some supersuccessful freelance photographer, and she agreed to critique my work. She's in town next week, so I'm showing it to her then. I'm almost done, too. I got so many great pictures in Cabo."

"So does that mean we can stay out here longer?" asked Blake. "Because there's this great ten-hour hike that I'd love to do, but we won't have time if we have to pack up and leave by sundown tomorrow."

"Sorry," said Cameron. "But I need to get back to LA."

"You're sure you can't stay for just one extra night?"

"I have this thing I have to go to. A doctor's appointment."

Actually, Cameron's next appointment was an entire week away, and it annoyed her that Blake made her have to lie.

"Is there something wrong?" he asked.

"No. It's nothing serious, but I'm having surgery in a few weeks."

Blake studied her face, clearly alarmed. "What's wrong?" he asked.

"Nothing." Cameron kicked at the ground. Her new hiking boots were already covered in red dust.

"No one has surgery for no reason."

"Don't worry, okay? I'm fine. I'm just getting a breast aug." It felt weird to say it out loud. Especially to Blake.

"A what?"

"A breast augmentation." Cameron shrugged one shoulder

casually, as if to communicate that it really wasn't a big deal. "I'm getting implants. Saline ones. It's just saltwater, really."

She hadn't planned on telling Blake during their trip, but it seemed silly to hide it. He was her boyfriend, and with the surgery just a couple of weeks away, he was going to find out soon enough.

"Very funny," said Blake.

"Seriously. I'm really doing it. Think of my body as a piece of art that I'm improving."

She tried walking past him, but he grabbed her wrist. "Wait a second. This is crazy. You're serious?"

Cameron nodded. She crossed her arms over her chest but quickly dropped them to her sides, not wanting to call attention to that area.

"You don't need implants."

"I never said I needed them. I'm doing this because I want to."

"But you're so beautiful."

"Well, there's nothing wrong with wanting to look better, right? I highlight my hair and tan and work out and wear makeup. You appreciate all of that, or you wouldn't be going out with me."

"I love you because of who you are." Blake seemed hurt, insulted even. "It's not because of what you look like. This all seems so fake."

"Okay," said Cameron. "But how come fake is bad? I mean, lots of things are fake. They carved out a niche in the desert where we camped. That's fake, right? And the road that we drove on to get here? There's nothing natural about that asphalt. Your backpack that you carry everywhere is made out of fake substances. The Nalgene bottle, our shoes . . ."

"You know what I mean. This is different. You're going through a completely unnecessary surgery with the sole purpose of altering your appearance. It's shallow, Cam."

"Well you're going out with me," she snapped. "So I guess we're both shallow."

"That's not fair."

"Or maybe you don't want me to look any better because you're afraid I'll meet someone else."

Blake's mouth twisted up in annoyance. "That's insane."

"You can't understand it, Blake, because you've always been beautiful, yet you don't even care. You've never had to struggle and you have no idea what I've been through, so you have no right to judge me."

He looked at her with narrowed eyes. "What are you talking about?"

Cameron didn't mean to shout but couldn't help herself. "When I lived in La Jolla, I was ugly, okay? I had a huge nose, but I had it fixed when I was fifteen. And I had braces, too, but they came off that same summer. And it was like I was a different person. You will never understand that, Blake, because you don't know how awful it is to look in the mirror and hate what you see. You don't know what it's like for people to tease you, to despise you, all because of what you look like."

"Okay, but aren't you pretty enough now?"

"That's not the point. I'm just fixing this one small flaw. It's not a big deal. Do you know how many cosmetic procedures were performed last year? Eleven-point-five million. In one year. It's not just me, Blake. Guess how much Americans spent on all those procedures? Twelve-point-four billion dollars."

"I don't care about the numbers," said Blake. "I care about you."

"If you cared, you'd be okay with this."

"That's not true. It's just so crazy."

"I'm not crazy. I'm human, and all humans are flawed. People make judgments based on the exterior. It's a fact of life. I'm not different from anyone else."

"Sure you are. Not everyone has plastic surgery."

"You never would have noticed me if I hadn't had my first surgery."

"That's so not true," Blake argued. "You don't know that."

"You have no idea what I know."

They continued to hike in silence. The sun beat down on their backs. Cameron was sweating in places she'd never sweat before, and she was grimy and coated in dust. Her hair had fallen out of its clip, but she didn't want to fix it because Blake might think *that* was shallow too, and she wasn't about to give him the satisfaction. She was too furious to look at him, and even too mad to stop and adjust her sock, which was bunching up on the outside of her left ankle and rubbing her skin raw.

"Hey, can we get out of here?" she asked, finally.

"Yeah, not fast enough." Blake pushed past her, continuing up the trail.

"Let's turn around, then."

"I told you before, we're hiking in a circle." Blake pointed to the trailhead in the not-so-far distance. "We're almost back."

"Good." Cameron held her breath, determined not to cry in front of Blake because he didn't deserve her tears.

"We'll be home before you know it," said Blake. "I know that's what you've wanted all along, anyway."

Cameron followed behind, silent but fuming. She couldn't argue. She did want to be back in LA. And she hadn't done anything but be brutally honest. There was nothing wrong with having cosmetic surgery. It wasn't her fault that the world was a shallow place. She had nothing to apologize for.

CHAPTER TEN

Wireless Internet access had come to the Motion Picture Home, and the residents greeted it with mixed emotions, confusion being the most common. On Monday, the beginning of Allie's second week there, she and the other volunteers were tasked with teaching everyone how to use it.

Since then, Allie had given a twenty-minute lecture on Web browsing. She'd helped a bunch of residents set up free e-mail accounts. And she'd pulled Nancy aside to suggest that Al get his own computer, so he could download pornography in the privacy of his room rather than in front of Bebe, who went to Catholic school and couldn't take that kind of thing. It had been a long week, and it was only Wednesday.

That afternoon they were doing individual tutoring sessions. Allie had started with a man named Herbert, but he'd fallen asleep on her after five minutes. Then she'd had Frank, whose hands shook so much, he couldn't use the keyboard himself. He'd been so frustrated with Allie's slow typing, he'd requested a new volunteer.

Now she was with Muriel, who had no interest in computers. If Allie didn't get through to her, the day would be a total failure.

"Now that you have an account, you can write to your granddaughter yourself," she tried.

Muriel hardly looked up from the book in her lap. "Tell her she needs to come visit."

"Don't you want to learn how to do this so you can tell her yourself?"

"Not particularly."

"I'm only here for another couple of weeks."

Muriel patted her arm and said, "There'll be other volunteers, dear."

It was hopeless. Allie looked around the room. Jenna was laughing with Sammy, an elderly comedian who used to appear on *The Tonight Show*. Allie didn't know what they were doing, but obviously Jenna was way ahead of her, since Sammy was actually looking at his computer screen. Bebe sat one station over, teaching Mrs. Campbell how to play bridge online.

Allie took one more stab. "It's not that hard."

"I have survived eighty-eight years without the Wonderful World of the Web machine. I think I will be okay without it now."

"It's actually the World Wide Web," said Allie. "And it's not exactly a machine. You were at the introduction lecture, right?"

"I must have fallen asleep."

"It's really easy to figure out, and you'll want to know how in the long run."

"Ha." Muriel waved her hand with such a flourish that her bracelets clashed against each other. "In the long run I'll be dead. Until then, you can e-mail my granddaughter for me. Tell her next Thursday is good, but it has to be after one, because I have a Scrabble game in the morning and they're serving broccoli quiche for lunch. I hate missing the quiche."

Turning back to the computer, Allie did as she was told.

"So how is everything going over here?" asked Nancy, walking over and smiling down at them.

Miserable, Allie thought but didn't say.

"Wonderful," said Muriel. "We were just finishing up. I'm so tired. I'd like to lie down for a bit."

"Okay, I'll take you back to your room," said Nancy.

Another one bites the dust, thought Allie, who felt bad almost as soon as the thought crossed her mind. Biting the dust had bad connotations at an old-age home.

"Allie, will you please get Eve?" Nancy asked. "She was supposed to be here for the tutorial, but she convinced Jenna that she was allergic to the moss that's growing in the walls."

"There's moss in these walls?" asked Allie.

"Of course not," said Nancy.

"If Eve is coming, then I'm glad I'm leaving," said Muriel. "I don't need to see Mrs. Big Movie Star Too Good for Hollywood and Too Good for the Rest of Us."

"Now, Muriel, that's not nice," said Nancy.

"But it's true," Muriel replied.

Nancy turned to Allie. "If she refuses to come, will you spend some time with her? She's been by herself all day, and it's just not healthy."

"Okay." Allie was happy to be released from the technology center, even if it meant spending time with Eve, who wasn't exactly pleasant, or even nice.

Allie hadn't seen her since their first meeting, but she'd watched all her old movies and had heard plenty of stories from her mom. In the course of her career, Eve had starred in five films, won two Academy Awards, dated three of her leading men, and then vanished just before her twenty-ninth birthday, at the height of her career. Allie was amazed, not that Eve had managed to disappear, but that she'd wanted to. What could motivate someone to give up what so many other people dreamed about?

When Allie got to bungalow seventeen, she knocked on the door.

"Who is it?" Eve called from inside.

"It's me, Allie. We met last week when I brought you to the screening of *Gone with the Wind*?"

"And what did I say about making statements in the form of a question?" asked Eve.

Allie was surprised that Eve remembered her. Or maybe she said that to all the volunteers. Allie would have to check with Bebe and Jenna. "I haven't forgotten. May I come in?"

"As I've said before, I can't stop you."

Walking inside, Allie found the living room empty. "Eve?" she called.

"I'm in the bedroom."

Allie walked through the door opposite the kitchen and saw Eve lying on a four-poster bed, looking small and birdlike in a pale cotton robe and matching cap.

"Nancy wanted me to get you. I'm doing technology tutoring today, if you're interested in learning more about the Internet . . ."

Eve closed her eyes. "Do I look like I'm interested in that?"

"You don't have to come." There was no place for her to sit, so Allie leaned against the wall. "We can just hang out here."

"'Hang out,'" Eve repeated under her breath.

"I know you'd rather be alone and I'm sorry about this," said Allie. "It wasn't my idea."

"Oh, I know. Nancy has been on my case ever since I got to this dreadful place. She wants me to socialize with the others." Eve said "socialize" as if it were a dirty word.

"If you hate it so much, why did you move here?" Allie hadn't meant to ask so blatantly, but it was the obvious question.

"It was an accident," said Eve. "I came to Los Angeles for a short visit but then broke my hip at the airport on the day I was supposed to fly back to Paris. When I was in the hospital I got pneumonia and the doctor wouldn't let me travel. I came here to recuperate. That was over a year ago. I'm not sure if I'll ever make it back home, so I had some of my things sent over, a few months ago."

"Is that where you've been all this time, Paris?"

Eve shook her head. "I've been in lots of places."

"And you swore you'd never come back to LA, right?"

"How do you know that?" asked Eve.

"My mom told me."

Eve closed her eyes. Allie thought she was going to sleep and wondered if she should leave the room, but then Eve spoke up. "I didn't want to come back here, but my friend died. She wanted her ashes to be scattered in the Pacific Ocean, in Malibu by the old Getty Museum. She was very specific."

"No one else could do it?" asked Allie.

"She was *my* friend. I wouldn't trust anyone else," Eve replied softly. Turning her head slowly, she looked at Allie. "And why are you here?"

"You already guessed it last week, remember? I have a community-service requirement at my school. They think it'll make our college applications look better."

"But why here?" asked Eve. "You don't seem to enjoy working with the elderly."

Allie couldn't deny it, and even if she tried, Eve wasn't going to believe her. "I wanted to work at this soccer camp for underprivileged kids, but the timing didn't work out, so my mom found me this. Nancy was really flexible when it came to my hours here."

"You play soccer?"

Allie nodded.

"And you like it?"

"I love it."

"What else do you love?" asked Eve. "Art?"

"Not really," said Allie.

"But the other day you said you liked the paintings on my walls. Were you lying?"

"Not at all," said Allie. "I think they're amazing."

"So you don't consider them art?"

"No, I . . ."

Worried she'd offended Eve, Allie didn't know what to say. Then she saw the small smile on Eve's cracked lips and realized she was being teased.

"I like art, in itself. I just don't like looking at things in museums. Any place where I have to stay cooped up inside and keep my voice down bugs me."

"Like an old-age home?"

"Kind of," Allie had to admit.

Eve laughed. "I appreciate your honesty, Allie. Those other volunteers are so cheerful all the time. Either they're completely insincere or there's something wrong with them."

"I like Jenna and Bebe. They're nice."

"Sure, to you," said Eve. "But to me they speak too slowly,

and in loud voices as if I were dumb and deaf. I can't stand it. You're different—genuine because you have to be."

"What do you mean, I have to be?"

"You're the type of person who can't hide from herself, and I like that. It's obvious to me that you dread being here, and we just met."

"I wouldn't say 'dread.' It's not *that* bad. I'm only here for another couple of weeks, anyway."

"What will you do afterward? Play soccer?"

"No."

"Well, why not?"

It was a fair question, but Allie had no intention of answering it. She pushed herself off the wall so she was standing upright. "Are you sure you don't want to learn how to use the computer?"

Eve's eyelids fluttered, like she was struggling to keep them open.

"Are you tired?" asked Allie. "Should I leave so you can get some sleep?"

"Yes, I think so."

As Allie left the bedroom, Eve called out to her. "You should always do what you love, Allie."

Allie turned around, asking, "Is that why you started acting?"

"It is," Eve replied. "And it's also why I stopped."

CHAPTER ELEVEN

"Do you understand what's involved in this procedure?" asked Dr. Glass.

Cameron squirmed under his gaze. He was good-looking, for an old guy. Plastic surgeons had to be, she guessed, since they were in the business of making people beautiful. She knew that he was married to a supermodel. Rumor had it he did all of her surgeries himself. Lots of actresses too.

Cameron wondered what he thought of her. What imperfections he noticed that would remain unvoiced because she was the daughter of his friend. Yes, friend. Cameron had just found out that her dad and Dr. Glass golfed at the same country club. Having her dad discuss her chest with some other man was almost too humiliating to think about, yet he must have done it, because here they were. Her dad had set up the extra appointment, and she wasn't happy about it. She'd already jumped through all of her parents' hoops. She'd outlined all the risks and had looked into the work-study program at UCSB just in case she failed to maintain a high enough GPA. Yet he still interfered.

"I've done a ton of research," said Cameron. "I know all about the risks."

"Good." Dr. Glass nodded. "Let me walk you through the procedure, then. The implants I use are saline, which is essentially saltwater, wrapped in a silicone case. If the saline leaks, it's not a problem, but you'll need another surgery to replace them. I'll cut a small half circle around the bottom of your nipple and insert the implant through there. Scarring will be minimal. The first twenty-four to forty-eight hours after breast augmentation surgery will be uncomfortable. You will probably experience pain and a lot of pressure, but that can be regulated with medication. You'll leave the surgi-center with a surgical bra, which you'll have to wear at all times. After a few days you'll come back here and I'll remove the bra and the bandages. Then we'll put Steri-Strips on your stitches. They're essentially small Band-Aids that will fall off in time. Your stitches will dissolve in ten days to two weeks. The scars will be hard and pink for about six weeks, and after that time, they may appear to widen. Then they'll fade over time, but they will never disappear completely."

"Yes," said Cameron. "I've read all about that."

"You may experience a burning sensation in your nipples

for about two weeks after the surgery," Dr. Glass continued. "And for three to four weeks following the procedure, your breasts will be extremely sensitive. You may have numbness in your nipple area, and there's a chance that the numbness will last forever. The opposite can happen, too. Your breasts may become extra sensitive, even painful to the touch. And again, this should go away, but it also may last forever. I can't make any guarantees because everyone is different."

"I know all this," said Cameron.

"Right, but I promised your father that I'd go over it all with you before agreeing to do the surgery."

Cameron crossed her arms over her chest. "That's so unfair. I'm a legal adult."

"It would be unethical if I didn't go over everything with you. And while at eighteen you're technically an adult, I usually don't perform this type of surgery on people so young."

"I won't be talked out of this."

"I'm aware of that," said Dr. Glass. "And it's not my intention, anyway. I just want you to understand what you're getting into. And I also need to ask you why you want to do this."

"Why does anyone have cosmetic surgery?" asked Cameron with a shrug. "I want to look better. You're in the business of making people beautiful, right?"

"You're already a beautiful young woman," Dr. Glass replied.

"Thanks to you." Cameron tossed her hair over one shoulder. It made her feel good that he'd called her beautiful, but also annoyed that she cared. "Anyway, lots of your patients are already beautiful, I'll bet. But that's not the only reason I'm having this procedure. I feel uneven, too bottom-heavy. Clothes don't fit me right."

Cameron was embellishing because she knew that when surgeons were dealing with teenagers, they were supposed to go through a list of questions. The answers she repeated were the acceptable ones. "Look what my nose job did for my self-esteem," she said, since "self-esteem" was listed as a good reason to have cosmetic surgery. "I was so self-conscious before, it was hard to function, but it changed my whole life."

"Most implants last seven to twelve years," said Dr. Glass. "Some last fifteen years, and some rupture or leak after just a few months or a few years."

"I've read that they can last longer," said Cameron. "Twenty-five years, even."

"Maybe, but it's not likely. You understand that this isn't a one-time deal? That you will have to go through surgery again, probably more than once, over the course of your lifetime?"

"Yes," said Cameron. "I'm prepared for that."

"They can also cause a rash or infection right away," said Dr. Glass. "It's very rare, but some women have allergic reactions to the silicone shell."

Cameron didn't need to hear this from Dr. Glass. "Like I said, I've done the research. Would you like me to tell you the risks?" Pulling her notebook from her purse, she began rattling off information to Dr. Glass.

"Capsular contracture is the most common complication in breast augmentation. It happens when scar tissue builds up and hardens around the implant. It feels tight and uncomfortable. It makes the breast too hard, and can also cause it to change its shape. Infection usually occurs within one to six weeks after surgery. In some cases, the implant will need to be removed and the patient treated with antibiotics. Hematoma, or an accumulation of blood near the surgical site, can occur, making it necessary for the surgeon to go in and drain the excess blood."

Cameron looked up. She kept waiting for Dr. Glass to stop her, but now she realized he wanted her to read the whole thing. *Fine,* she thought. It wasn't going to make her change her mind.

"Some women say they can hear the saline swish whenever they move, and I know that implants don't warm up the way natural breasts do. So when I go skiing, my breasts will feel colder than the rest of my body. Breast implants can interfere with mammography, a test to screen for tumors, especially if there is capsular contracture. Also, rippling can occur when the saline shifts within the implant."

She lowered the paper and looked at Dr. Glass. "Happy?" she asked.

"Studies by implant manufacturers report that most women have at least one serious complication within the first three years," he said. "In my experience, complications have been minor, but they can include any or all of those you listed."

"How many of your patients regret what you've done to them?" asked Cameron.

"Ten percent come in for more surgery," Dr. Glass replied.

"But how many ask you to take their implants out?"

"Honestly, not so many."

"So that means most of your breast augmentation patients are happy with the results?"

Dr. Glass nodded. "Yes, they are. But most are also older than you. Those your age, well, they're usually doing it for their career. But your dad tells me you have no interest in the entertainment industry."

Cameron bristled. Was he acknowledging that she had no intention, or that she had no choice because she hadn't a chance? And what did that matter, anyway? Surely being better-looking would help her in any career. Why was that so hard for people to admit?

"I'm going to double major in photography and business,"

said Cameron. "I like to take pictures, and I don't see why I can't look as great as my subject matter. Better, even."

Dr. Glass nodded. "If you are as determined in your career as you are in this endeavor, I have a feeling you'll be very successful."

"So you'll do it?" asked Cameron.

"I understand that you'll be getting implants with or without me."

"Yes. The other doctor wanted to put them in through an incision near my belly button so the scars wouldn't show."

Dr. Glass cringed. "That's a bad surgery. Don't do that."

"I'd rather go with you, anyway."

"You won't wait a year to think about it?"

"A year will be too late," said Cameron. "I'm starting college in September. I'll be meeting all these new people and I don't want anyone to know."

Dr. Glass nodded. Leaning forward, he looked at his appointment book. "I have room in my schedule in a few weeks. On a Thursday, actually. The same day I'm doing your sister and your mom."

"My mom?" asked Cameron. "What do you mean?"

Dr. Glass picked up his phone and pressed a button. "Madison, please send in Julie Davenport and Allie Beekman."

He hung up, took off his glasses and rubbed the bridge of his nose.

Cameron thought that Dr. Glass must have made a mistake. "My mom isn't having surgery," she said.

"You mean she hasn't told you?"

"What's she doing?"

"Why don't you wait a minute," said Dr. Glass. "So she can tell you herself."

CHAPTER TWELVE

"A face-lift is a really big deal, isn't it?" asked Allie.

"Why would you say that?" asked Cameron.

"Because it's Mom's face."

Julie was sitting right across from her, but Allie was too embarrassed to question her directly. And even though she and Cameron were whispering, their mom still asked them to keep it down. They were in public, after all, at Sushi Hanna on Melrose Boulevard. The three of them shared a table for four. On the empty plate sat a manila envelope containing the digital-imaging shots of the postsurgical, new and improved mother and daughters.

In a sense it was a relief to Allie. All this time she'd thought there was something wrong with her. It comforted her to know that she wasn't the only one in need of fixing. It made her feel less alone, but it also worried her. Julie and Cameron were beautiful, no question. So if they thought they needed surgery, what did that say about all the regular people like Allie? How much would her nose improve her looks? Would she need more surgery later on? Was it like an addiction? Would it be impossible to stop? And what if she didn't even like her nose in the end? What would happen then? Of course, if she loved it, what would that say about her? And what would it do to her? Would she start taking an hour and a half to get ready for school every morning? What did her sister do with all that time, anyway?

Allie felt nervous for Cameron. Even though she insisted that she didn't want huge boobs, Allie couldn't help but think of Pamela Anderson.

Then there was her mother. Allie had seen plenty of pictures of women with bad face-lifts, their skin pulled back so much that it looked shiny and tight. Her friend Carly's mom resembled a cat. Sure, Julie had a few wrinkles, but Allie hadn't even noticed them until her mom pointed them out. And to be honest, now that she could tell, Allie liked that her mom looked soft and real in a city where so much was hard and fake.

"What does Dad think?" asked Allie.

"He says I don't need it, which is very sweet, but he's not the reason I want this. I'm doing it for my career and for myself." Julie straightened the crisp white napkin on her lap. "I'm turning forty-five in a few weeks, you know. I thought, why not give myself a birthday gift?"

"So you think it'll help you get work?" asked Cameron.

Their mom sighed. "I hope so. Not having a face-lift certainly isn't doing anything for me."

"But you just started auditioning again," said Allie.

"I've been thinking about doing this for a long time. I'm competing with women who are half my age. Girls who are your age, even."

"Isn't it dangerous, all of us doing this on the same day?" asked Allie.

Julie smiled. "Honey, stop worrying. It will be easier because I've hired a private nurse to take care of us."

"Well, what if there's a bad batch of anesthesia? It could wipe us all out, and then Dad will be left alone." Allie bit back her tears.

"I don't think anesthesia comes in batches, sweetie," Julie said.

Cameron laughed. "Don't stress about this, Allie. Dr. Glass does families all the time. He told me he once did breast augmentation on twins, and he knows a guy who did rhinoplasty on triplets, two sisters and a brother, all in the same day."

"I just don't think Mom should do this," said Allie. She grinned at her mom, apologetically.

"That's kind of hypocritical, don't you think?" asked Cameron. "I mean, we're all doing it."

Allie knew that arguing with her sister would be pointless. When Cameron wanted something, she was ruthless about getting it. Everyone knew that. Allie admired her sister's determination, but she also found it intimidating.

As Allie looked away, a hunky waiter approached.

"Hello, ladies," he said as he sidled up to the table. His tanned biceps seemed perpetually flexed, and his dark, shiny eyes crinkled in the corners. He smiled so radiantly, he reminded Allie of some guy in a movie—a struggling actor playing the part of a waiter.

Cameron tucked her hair behind her ear and Julie smiled up at him.

"So, three sisters out for lunch?" he asked, winking at Cameron. It was a cheesy line and they all knew it, but that didn't mean that their mom didn't appreciate it. Allie was just glad he'd said three sisters rather than two sisters and one big-nosed, dark-haired troll.

"Can I start you off with some drinks?" he asked. "The passionfruit iced tea is amazing."

"I'll try that," said Julie.

"Me too," said Cameron.

"I'll have a lemonade," Allie said.

"You know what I was thinking?" asked Cameron, as soon as the waiter left. "It's good that we all have the same surgeon, because we'll still look like a family."

"Except for Dad," said Allie.

"That's not true. We've got Dad's dark hair," said Cameron. Then, grinning, she added, "Well, you do and I did."

"Both of you girls have your father's smile," said their mom. "And your father's brains. That's what really matters."

It was nice of her to say, but Allie didn't think she meant it. How could she, when Allie's grades were so rotten? Cameron got their mom's looks and their dad's brains, so what did that leave for Allie?

Cameron grabbed her hand. "Allie, promise me that when it's time for us to get face-lifts, we'll find the same surgeon so we'll still look like sisters, okay? I'm sure Dr. Glass will be retired by then."

"We hardly look like sisters now," Allie pointed out.

"Well, we will in a few weeks."

When the waiter came back with their drinks, he said to Cameron, "I feel like a tool for asking you this, but I can't help it. You look so familiar. Have I seen you on the Warner Brothers lot, maybe? Because you look like an actress."

"I'm not," said Cameron, smiling and sitting up straighter. "But my mom is."

"Really?" He turned to Julie, his smile fading ever so slightly as he tried to place her.

Julie bit her bottom lip and studied the menu, even though she always ordered the same thing at sushi restaurants.

"What were you in?" he asked.

"Nothing much," said Julie. "It was a long time ago."

"She starred in *The Deepest Bluest Sea*," said Cameron.

The waiter shrugged. "I haven't seen so many old movies."

Then, realizing his faux pas, he said, "I mean, not old. I haven't seen so many movies, at all."

No one said anything.

"What can I get you for lunch?" he asked, looking down at his notepad.

Julie ordered her usual in a clipped voice: seaweed salad, tuna and salmon sashimi, and an eel-cucumber roll. Cameron had the same. Not one for raw fish, Allie asked for the chicken teriyaki.

All three of them were relieved when the waiter went away. No one commented on the fact that a different waiter brought out their food, or that the original guy stayed exiled on the other side of the patio for the rest of their meal.

Allie watched him from across the restaurant. Her mom used to be the one waiters flirted with. Now it was her sister. When had that changed? And was this why her mother wanted a face-lift?

Cameron placed the manila envelope on her lap and peeked inside. "It's amazing how natural it all looks," she said.

Julie leaned over so she could see the pictures, too. "People call Dr. Glass the Michelangelo of plastic surgeons," she said.

"They say that about practically every plastic surgeon," said Allie.

"How do you know?" asked Cameron.

"I've been reading about it online," Allie replied as she glanced at the shots.

In the picture, Cameron's boobs looked perfect, Allie's nose was straight and cute, and Julie looked like she did in her wedding pictures, twenty years before.

Despite her reluctance, Allie had to admit that they all looked beautiful, like better versions of themselves. Not like other people, as she'd feared. And while Dr. Glass had said that the pictures were a mere representation of what he could do under ideal circumstances, rather than a guarantee, it was hard not to see it that way.

The human body rendered as a lump of clay, merely a template for something better.

Before they left the restaurant, Julie and Cameron stopped in the restroom to fix their makeup. Allie waited by the door, observing all the tanned, pretty people in expensive-looking clothes walk by. The food at Sushi Hanna was good, but Allie dreaded eating there. The place made her feel trapped in a game at which everyone else excelled, while she couldn't quite figure out the rules. Perhaps she'd feel differently in a few weeks. Maybe it was like a club, and once her nose was fixed, she'd be asked to join.

"Excuse me," someone said from behind her. "Can I ask you a question?"

Allie turned around to find their original waiter peering down at her. He was even better-looking close-up. She couldn't help but smile at him. "You just did, but go ahead and ask me another."

He handed Allie a scrap of paper. "Can you give your sister my number? I'd love to take her out sometime."

Allie kept her smile frozen on her face and took the scrap. "Sure," she said.

This type of thing had happened before, so she wasn't surprised.

What shocked her was the thought that popped into her head as she watched him walk away: If the waiter had seen her postsurgery, might he have given his number to her, instead?

CHAPTER THIRTEEN

Ashlin sat on the floor of her bedroom with Cameron's red, leather-bound portfolio in her lap. Lucy and Hadley were on either side of her, leaning in close so they could get a better look at the pictures.

It always gave Cameron such a rush, watching people admire her work. Although this time it wasn't exactly a surprise, since her friends were the subject matter and she'd made them all look gorgeous.

In a sense, she owed it to them. They'd all been great about helping her out in Cabo. After being so supportive and understanding about the evil La Jolla crowd, they'd spent countless hours posing—leaning on the rocks by the beach, rolling around in the sand, frolicking ankle-deep in the surf, and lounging by the pool. Cameron had done group shots and individual portraits, and the final result was impressive. She had a series of thirty stunning pictures, all laid out and ready to send to David Champlain. Half were in color and half were black and white. The more artistic shots came toward the end: Ashlin's bare foot half covered in sand, two points from a starfish in one corner of the frame. Hadley staring pensively out to sea as her blond hair whipped in the wind.

Looking through it gave her a thrill, mostly because her friends were so beautiful. They were the proof that Cameron had succeeded, that she'd moved beyond the girl she once was.

"I must get a copy of this one," said Lucy, pointing to the close-up of her face and torso. In it, she was grinning slyly as she emerged from the pool. Water droplets cascaded from her dark hair. Cameron felt especially proud of that shot, since photographing water was such a challenge. She had aimed for the style of a classic pinup. Lucy's cleavage looked so amazing, Cameron had made an extra print to bring to Dr. Glass. She decided that she wanted breasts that were as natural as Lucy's—the same shape, but just a tad larger.

"I'll print one out for you later."

"What are you guys looking at?" asked Taylor, as she walked into the room and set her purse on the floor.

"Oh my gosh. Let me see!" Hadley cried, jumping up and rushing over to her friend. She put a hand on each of Taylor's shoulders and peered at her face.

"What's she looking at?" Cameron asked.

Lucy shrugged. "I don't know."

"Anyone notice anything different?" asked Hadley, placing her arm around Taylor and grinning like crazy.

"Don't tell them. I want to see if they can guess," Taylor said.

Cameron had no idea what was going on. Neither did Ashlin or Lucy. Hadley had been clued in earlier and couldn't stand the suspense. She cracked within seconds, blurting out, "Taylor just got permanent eyeliner tattoos."

Taylor's features crumpled in disappointment, forehead wrinkled, mouth pursed, eyebrows scrunched. "I wanted them to guess," she cried.

"They were never going to. It's way too subtle," Hadley said.

"Do you think I should have gone darker? My mom thought it would be a good base for every day, and this way I can always color over it."

Cameron moved closer and studied the thin ring of light brown circling each of Taylor's eyes. The perfectly symmetrical lines got thicker toward the outside edges. "It looks great," she said. "Totally glamorous."

Taylor's entire face lit up. "Thanks."

"Did you get that done in Vegas?" asked Ashlin.

Taylor nodded. "That's partly why we went. My mom knows a makeup artist up there. This was my graduation gift."

"Is it really permanent?" asked Lucy.

"Not exactly," said Taylor. "It'll last a few years, though." Noticing the portfolio in Ashlin's arms she asked, "Are those pictures from Cabo? I want to see."

Ashlin handed over the book and Taylor flipped through it quickly—too quickly, in Cameron's opinion. "These are great," she said, as she set the book down on Ashlin's desk. "But I thought you were going to take pictures of Blake out in Joshua Tree."

Cameron groaned. Everyone else knew better than to bring him up, but apparently news of the fight hadn't made it to Taylor.

"We're not exactly talking at the moment." Cameron kept things vague, but Taylor wasn't going to let her off the hook so easily.

"What happened?" she asked.

"Yeah, you never told us any of the gory details," said Lucy.

There was a reason for that. If Cameron told her friends about the fight, she'd have to tell them everything, and she felt weird about it. Of course, she didn't have much of a choice now. They were all staring at her, waiting, and it wasn't like they weren't going to find out soon enough, anyway.

"It's complicated," said Cameron, sitting down on Ashlin's bed and leaning against the headboard. "Basically, I'm getting breast implants in a couple of weeks, and when I told Blake, he freaked out and called me shallow."

Lucy screamed. "Oh my gosh. Cam, you're kidding."

Cameron shook her head. "Seriously. I've been thinking about this for ages. You guys know how self-conscious I am about my chest, right? Well, I finally decided to do something about it."

"That's awesome," said Taylor. "How big are you going to go?"

"Nothing crazy. I want to be a C cup."

"Wait, didn't all those women get sick from breast implants?" asked Lucy. "Don't they leak poison?"

"Those were the old kind," said Cameron. "They were filled with silicone, but now they're made with saline. If they leak it's not a big deal, because the liquid will just get absorbed into your body. It's only saltwater—totally harmless."

"But isn't the shell still silicone?" asked Lucy.

"Technically, yes," said Cameron.

"And don't they still leak?" asked Ashlin.

"Sometimes," said Cameron. "Rarely."

"Are you sure you want to do this?" asked Ashlin. "You totally don't need them."

"I never said I needed them. I just want them." Cameron shrugged and ran her hand through her hair. "Anyway, it's not so different from tattooed eyeliner."

"True," said Taylor.

"It's totally different," said Ashlin. "The tattoos fade, but you're putting these foreign things into your body permanently. It's way more dangerous and . . . just so fake."

"Really?" asked Cameron, raising her eyebrows and staring pointedly at her friend. "It's so interesting that you're calling me fake, Ms. LASIK Surgery who's been getting her hair straightened for four years."

"Ouch," said Ashlin. "No need to be mean about it."

"I'm just sick of everyone being so negative about this whole thing. You have no idea what I've had to go through with my parents."

"I can't believe they're letting you do it," said Lucy.

"I'm an adult, so they have no choice," said Cameron. "Anyway, it's not that big of a deal. And Ashlin, look what plastic surgery did for that character in that novel you lent me."

"*Flavor of the Month*? Cameron, do you know what happened to the woman who wrote that book?" asked Ashlin. "Olivia Goldsmith went in for some simple plastic surgery and it killed her."

"Come on," said Cameron.

"Seriously. She slipped into a coma after they gave her anesthesia and she never woke up."

Suddenly Cameron had the chills. "No way. That's a total urban myth."

"It's true. Look it up," said Ashlin.

"I will, but I'm telling you, I've done so much research into this, and sure, there are some risks, but most women are totally fine after. It's totally worth it. My doctor said they're perfectly safe and he wouldn't lie."

"So what did Blake say?" asked Lucy.

"At this point, I can't even remember. I'm still traumatized by our miserable ride home from Joshua Tree. We didn't say a word to each other for the entire three hours. I've never seen him so mad."

"It's a crazy thing to break up over," said Lucy. "I mean, it's sort of sweet in a way. He's upset that you want to change yourself. It's like he's saying that he loves you the way you are."

"But I was never doing this for him in the first place. The assumption is so arrogant. It's my decision and he should be supportive. I respect Blake and all of his beliefs. I never make fun of him when he wears that stupid beret, and last winter I helped him organize the boycott of the school cafeteria after he found out they were buying their chickens from factory farms."

Ashlin and Lucy looked at each other. "It's a little different," said Ashlin.

Cameron was annoyed. "Is it, though? No one thought there was anything terrible about my getting a nose job, so why are people freaking out now? It's not like I'm mainlining crack."

"Let's not fight. This is stupid," said Lucy. "Are we going out to lunch or what?"

"Finally. I'm starving," said Taylor.

"I'll drive," said Hadley.

As everyone filed out of the room, Cameron grabbed her portfolio off Ashlin's desk. "I'll catch up with you guys later. I have to go."

"Are you sure?" asked Ashlin.

Cameron nodded. No way was she going to stick around. Ashlin's outright disapproval was annoying enough, but Lucy's failure to defend her somehow felt even worse. Who were they to act like she was doing some horrible, scandalous thing? Everyone wanted to look as good as they could. She wasn't guilty of being anything but human.

CHAPTER FOURTEEN

As Allie circled the empty parking lot for the third time, she felt like a Motion Picture Home resident driving one of their battery-operated golf carts. Her hands gripped the steering wheel in the three and nine o'clock positions, just like she'd been taught in driver's ed. Except she was holding on too tightly, and her shoulders were tensed up practically to her ears. Also, she leaned too far forward and squinted out at the road too intensely.

"I think you're ready for the street," said her dad, despite her obvious flaws.

"Tell that to Brian Hughes," Allie replied.

"Who?"

"The guy whose car I wrecked."

"It was an accident," said her dad, with the wave of one hand. "It could've happened to anyone."

"But it happened to me," Allie reminded him.

"You need to put that behind you. That guy's a jerk, driving around in a gas guzzler like that. And you learned your lesson, so I'm glad you hit him!"

Her father's kindness made Allie feel worse. It was as if she had failed him once more but he didn't mind because he hadn't expected anything better from her.

She circled the parking lot again, carefully watching everything in front of her. There wasn't much to see but pavement and white lines, but that was sort of the point.

"Seriously, hon. Turn right out of the exit. You can do this."

"Am I boring you?" asked Allie.

"Honestly? Yes, but that's not why I'm asking you to drive in traffic. You have to get over this fear. So, let's take Mulholland Boulevard."

"The canyon?" Allie pressed on the brakes and shifted the car into park. "No, that road has way too many curves."

"But not much traffic at this hour," Jeffrey countered. "So let's go."

Sighing, Allie did as she was told. And once she got over the initial nervousness, it wasn't so horrible to be on the road. The leathery smell of her dad's car felt comforting, as did the gentle hum of the air-conditioning. She was used to this car and she liked it.

It felt good to be out of the house, too. Ever since Cameron had come home early from Joshua Tree, things had been kind of tense. She and their dad still hardly spoke. Cameron did everything she could to avoid him, spending all her time in her room working on her portfolio, or out with her friends. Blake stopped coming around, and Allie missed him. She asked her sister what was going on, but Cameron refused to talk about it.

Only this morning before the driving lesson had she actually said a word to Allie. Cameron was convinced that her decision to get breast implants was no more significant than Allie's nose job, and she wanted Allie to say as much to their father. Allie wasn't sure she agreed, but she promised to have the conversation.

Not that she could think of any natural way to bring it up. "So, um, surgery day isn't too far away," said Allie. It was a weak attempt but it worked.

Her father grunted. "And what do you think of Cameron's plans?"

"She doesn't think it's that big of a deal," said Allie. "She's already been through surgery once and it worked out pretty well . . ."

"And what do you think?"

Allie shrugged. "It's weird, I guess. Although it is about Mom, too."

"That's different," said Jeffrey. "Your mother is an adult, and she's had a rough time, you know. It's been a long struggle."

"What has?" asked Allie.

"Going back to work."

"But she's just started auditioning."

Jeffrey shook his head. "It's a tough business for older women. And your mother is being very realistic about the whole thing. She isn't even going out for lead roles. She'd be more than happy to land something small—a supporting part in a sitcom, or a low-budget movie—but even that's impossible. After all that rejection, I can see why she'd want to do something like this."

Allie had never thought of her mother as someone who'd ever struggled for anything. She hadn't even realized that Julie wanted to act that badly; she'd always thought her mom's renewed interest was more of a hobby, like the organic gardening she'd taken up a few months ago, and the knitting before that. If she'd really loved acting so much, why had she given it up in the first place?

"I had no idea," said Allie.

"Don't tell her I said anything. She doesn't want you girls to worry about her. Anyway, it's your sister with the bigger problem. I don't understand why this is so important to her."

"It's weird, but I feel like a hypocrite for saying anything, since I'm having surgery, too."

"Don't worry. A nose job isn't a big deal. I feel bad that you girls inherited more of my looks than you did your mother's. It's like I owe you a better nose."

At the next light, Allie glanced at her father's familiar

profile. His nose was large and hooked, much bigger than hers, yet she'd never heard him mention it before. "If you think your nose is too big, how come you never got it fixed?"

Her father grinned. "I see what you're getting at, Allie, and you have a good point. We live in a superficial world, and it's much harder for women. The double standard isn't fair or right, but that's how it is. Sure, I wish I was better-looking, but my nose certainly didn't affect my life the way it did Cameron's. Maybe you're too young to remember, but your sister was very unhappy before we left La Jolla. Junior high was especially hard for her."

What Allie remembered about La Jolla was that back then, Cameron was always so much more available. She used to buy Allie Barbie dolls, even though Allie never cared for them. What she loved was playing with her big sister, watching Cameron pose the dolls and take their pictures. She'd make up elaborate stories about them, pretending that Malibu Barbie was the head of an international modeling agency. In Cameron's world, Ken wasn't Barbie's boyfriend. He was her assistant.

Everything changed after they moved. Cameron was older, and she started dressing herself up, posing for self-portraits, and taking pictures of her friends.

Allie always figured that Cameron lost interest in the Barbies because people were more interesting than plastic dolls. Now she realized that Cameron's focus had merely shifted. She'd once worked to make dolls look like people. Now she focused on making people look like dolls.

"Was her nose really that bad before?"

"It was like your nose," said Jeffrey. "So you tell me."

Her father's words were like a jellyfish sting, the pain stunning, yet the source untraceable. Her nose was big. She knew that. Just, why did that automatically mean she needed surgery? Lots of people had big noses. They didn't all get them fixed. Somehow people managed.

"I have to miss a week of soccer camp because I'll be recovering."

"Don't worry. A week won't set you back too much."

"Coach McAdams is bringing someone up to the varsity team, but if I miss a whole week of the camp she won't let me try out."

This was the first time Allie had voiced her concern out loud.

"That's not fair," said her dad. "You're the best on the JV team."

"Quincy scored more points last year."

"But you beat her with assists, and you're much better all around."

"If I decided not to get it done, would you be upset?"

"Of course not. It's your nose. You can always do it over Christmas vacation, or even next summer. I just assumed that you'd want to get it fixed as soon as you could."

"Why?" asked Allie.

She could hear her dad shift uncomfortably in his seat. "Cameron told us what your soccer teammates call you."

"Huh?"

"The Beak," he said softly.

Allie felt like laughing. "So?"

"Well, I'd be insulted if someone called me the Beak."

When the light turned green, Allie stepped on the gas pedal. "Our last name is Beekman. Everyone on the team has a nickname that's derivative of their last name."

"Oh."

"They don't say it to be mean."

"Of course not, honey. But doesn't it hurt, just a little? It's okay to tell me, you know. I understand that even the closest friends can be insensitive sometimes."

"Seriously, I never even thought about it like that."

Allie could tell that her father didn't believe her. It was absurd to argue, though. "Can we go home now?" she asked.

"Did I say something to upset you?"

Allie shook her head.

"All I want is for you to be happy."

Allie didn't doubt that this was the case. Rather, she hadn't realized she was unhappy. Or, at least, that everyone assumed she must be.

CHAPTER FIFTEEN

When Selby Chasen breezed into the Beekman house, the entire center of gravity seemed to shift so that all focus was on her and her alone.

"Julie Davenport!" she cried, air-kissing Cameron's mom on the cheek one, two, and then three times. "You look amazing."

"And you're a wonderful liar," Julie said, laughing and clearly pleased.

"You must be Cameron," said Selby, shaking her hand firmly. "You look just like your mom. I'm so excited to see your work. We should get to it, though. I only have fifteen minutes, because I have to meet my agent for lunch and then I'm flying to Fiji tonight."

"Fiji?" asked Cameron.

"I'm shooting some new Japanese rock band for *Rolling Stone*," Selby explained.

Selby worked as a freelance photographer based in San Francisco, but she traveled the world, specializing in photographing musicians. She'd even dated a couple of them. Her current boyfriend had two platinum albums and was ten years her junior. No huge shocker since Selby was so beautiful. She had pixie-like features, short dark hair, and large gray eyes. Although she couldn't have been more than five feet tall, she was bursting with enough energy to fill up the entire room.

Cameron was in awe.

"Why don't you two work in the dining room," said Julie, ushering Selby toward the back of the house. "Can I get you a drink?"

"No thanks," said Selby.

Once they were settled, Cameron handed over her portfolio. From everything she'd heard about her mom's friend, she knew she'd like Selby. What she hadn't counted on was this: She wanted Selby to like her work so much, it actually hurt.

Selby pored over the pages quietly and carefully.

Cameron waited, which was much more complicated than it sounded. She didn't know if she should look at her pictures with Selby, or if that would be considered rude, like reading over someone's shoulder. Although maybe it would be rude *not* to look, since Selby had taken time out of her busy schedule to do this.

Sneaking a peek at her watch, Cameron realized that six whole minutes had gone by and Selby had yet to say a word.

And what was she supposed to do with her hands? Clasping them in her lap kept them out of the way, but she worried that it looked weird. Placing them on the edge of the table wasn't right, either. It made her feel like a puppy begging for scraps. Of course, scraps were essentially what she was after: a nod, a smile, the acknowledgment that she had talent or at least some potential—anything.

The problem was, seeing her pictures through Selby's gaze made them look so amateurish. The red portfolio seemed garish. Cameron saw flaws in her pictures that she hadn't noticed before: awkward poses, a cactus branch that looked as if it were coming out of Taylor's ear, a dark shadow in the corner of one of the group shots.

"There's a mistake in this one," Cameron blurted out, panicky and unable to stand the silence any longer. "I can fix it, though."

Selby nodded. "I'm sure you can. I can tell you really know what you're doing, technically."

"I just want to make sure that everything is perfect. The shoot took a while. My friends were ready to kill me, I think."

"I can tell." Selby pointed to the shot of Hadley looking out to sea. "She's smiling, but I can see that it's forced and that she's really annoyed. Look at the way the corners of her mouth are strained."

Cameron nodded. She hadn't even noticed that before. "I can find something better to replace that one."

"No, it's great. I like the emotion brewing underneath the surface. It makes it more interesting."

Cameron was both sorry that she'd said anything and thrilled that Selby had called one of her pictures great. Or was she merely referring to Hadley's expression?

Selby continued to flip through, pausing at the shot of Ashlin's bare toes and the starfish. "Now what were you trying to say here?"

Cameron stared at the shot. "I'm not sure what you mean."

"The composition is striking. I'm just wondering what you're going for."

"I guess I was focusing on the texture of the sand and I liked the way her toes looked, coming out of it." Cameron sensed that this answer was wrong, but it was the only one she had.

Selby closed the portfolio and smiled at Cameron. "Your technique is very good, Cameron. You have an innate sense of composition, which is wonderful. The beach scenes are beautiful, as are the young women you've chosen to photograph."

"Thanks." Cameron felt so relieved.

"I'm just not sure what you're trying to say," Selby added.

"Um, what do you mean?" asked Cameron.

"As you know, so much about the field of photography is

about selling things. Not just objects, but ideas and images, too. It's how I make my living, sadly. But you're trying to get into an art class, right? And art, to me, is about communication. You should strive to take pictures that transcend themselves, pictures that have a larger message, you know?"

Cameron didn't know but nodded anyway.

"When I'm looking at a piece of work, I want to be engaged, and at the very least I want to be made to think. As an artist, your goal is to convey some sort of message, to make a statement and inspire dialogue. I'm surprised this wasn't covered in your high school art classes."

Cameron felt the blood drain from her face. "So they're not that good?"

"Look, I don't want to upset you. These are fine pictures. Individually, there's very little to criticize. But taken as a whole? I'm left wondering what this is all about. You have lots of very sexualized pictures of young women, but what does that all add up to? Right now it's unclear, and you want to say *something*, right? Otherwise, how will you distinguish your work from the kind of thing that's published in those horrible lad magazines like *Maxim* or *FHM*?"

"My pictures are that bad?" Cameron felt her voice waver.

"No, but let me explain." Selby opened up the book and turned to the photograph of Lucy emerging from the water. "This one, for example. Your friend is beautiful, but so what? Is there another point? Because if not, it's like you're turning her into a commodity. She's being objectified, sold like a can of soda or a brand of cigarettes."

Cameron swallowed hard. "I guess I was just focused on getting the water drops in focus," she said weakly.

Selby nodded. "And you did a great job of that. Like I said, you seem to have mastered all the technical aspects of digital photography, which is no easy feat. Furthermore, I can tell that you've worked hard on these pictures, and I'm sure that will impress David Champlain."

"But you don't like my work. These aren't good enough, right? That's what you think."

Cringing, Selby opened her mouth to speak, but the words didn't come.

"Please be honest with me," said Cameron. "I can take it."

"I'm not crazy about them, but I'm just giving you my opinion, maybe something to think about. I can see that you're capable of doing more, and in the end it doesn't matter what I think. What's important is what you think, and that you think. So if I were you, I'd go back to the beginning. Decide what kind of message you want to send and then send it by making sure that every single image in your book says something about that original statement. Okay?"

"Sure, thanks," said Cameron, pulling her portfolio back. She jumped out of her chair. "I'll go get my mom. I'm sure she'll want to say good-bye. Um, it was nice meeting you. Good luck in Fiji. Thank you for looking at these."

"Good luck to you, too," said Selby.

Cameron bolted, happy that she made it out of the room before her tears started falling.

CHAPTER SIXTEEN

Allie ran up the canyon at Griffith Park as fast as she could. Without Quincy it was hard to gauge how fast she was actually going. All she knew was what she felt in her gut—she wasn't moving fast enough.

As soon as she made it to the top, she jogged back down to the halfway point, where the trail began to get steep. The sun beat down relentlessly. Sweat soaked Allie's T-shirt and dust coated her shoes and socks. She felt a blister forming on her big toe. Still, she pushed on, running up the hill because she needed to be faster than Quincy. If she wasn't going to be on varsity, then at least she'd be able to prove that she was good enough, that she could have played had she been allowed to try out.

After two more trips up, her body screamed at her to stop. Her mind tried to object, but her legs were about to give out on her. With her heart pounding and her eyes stinging from salty sweat, she limped home.

After showering and changing, Allie headed downstairs, moving carefully, because her muscles were already getting stiff and sore. She found her sister sitting cross-legged on the couch. Cameron had a stack of magazines piled on either side of her, and she was flipping through one furiously.

"So I take it you and Blake are still fighting?"

"How'd you guess?" asked Cameron, hardly looking up from her reading.

"It's eight o'clock on a Friday night and you're at home in dirty sweatpants."

"I'm pretty pathetic, huh?" asked Cameron.

"Guess I'm pathetic too, then," Allie replied.

"No, you're still young. You're not expected to have big plans every weekend."

"Well that's a relief," said Allie.

"Plus, you're wearing clean clothes. Hey, are those my jeans?"

"You gave them to me last year."

Cameron was always giving Allie her old clothes and then forgetting about it. Allie was too tired to be annoyed this time. "What are you doing?" she asked.

"Shopping for my new boobs." Cameron pushed some of the magazines aside to make room on the couch for Allie. "Come look."

As Allie sat down next to her, Cameron flipped to a perfume ad. "What do you think of those?" She pointed to a model in long blond braids. She was splayed out on a rock and staring up at a guy who was wearing blue tights and a red velvet leotard thing with silver sequins. He had a feather in his cap. There was a white horse in the background.

"Is he supposed to be a prince or something?"

Cameron blew her bangs out of her face, clearly annoyed. "I mean, what do you think of her chest?"

"Are those fake?" asked Allie.

"Yes," said Cameron. "You can tell because they're not sagging to the side. Real boobs don't defy gravity like that."

Tilting her head, Allie looked again. "Don't you want something more natural-looking?"

"Probably." Cameron flipped to a different page. "Check out this shot of Jessica Simpson."

"I think they're too big, but it's hard to tell because she's wearing a sweater."

"I know. I really should get a *Playboy* or a *Penthouse* or something, but I can't imagine just walking into a store and buying one. It'd be so embarrassing, and what if I run into someone I know?"

"I think Mom has a Victoria's Secret catalog upstairs. Want me to get it?"

"That's okay. We have *Desperate Housewives* on TiVo."

"I saw one of them at Coffee Bean and Tea Leaf last week," said Allie.

"Which one?" asked Cameron.

"I don't know their real names."

"Was it her?" asked Cameron, showing Allie a page in *Entertainment Weekly*.

"Yes, but she doesn't look like that in person."

Cameron rolled her eyes. "Of course she doesn't. Don't you know how things work at magazines?" She had this way of asking questions that made Allie feel stupid for not already knowing the answers.

"What do you mean?"

"First they spend like four hours on hair and makeup, and then they make the lighting soft enough to accentuate curves and someone's best features, and they only shoot from certain angles. Once they take the pictures, they fix things on the computer. It's all airbrushing and Photoshop."

"Really?"

Cameron pointed to the woman on the cover of *Vogue*. The face was familiar, but Allie couldn't remember her name or even if she starred in movies or on TV.

"That's not really her," said Cameron. "After they took the picture, they made her skin smoother and her legs longer and her teeth whiter. Sometimes they'll shoot an actress and then replace her real body with the body of some skinnier model."

"Is that legal?" Allie picked up the magazine so she could get a closer look.

"Probably not, but who's going to complain when they look better this way?"

"So those pictures don't mirror reality at all?"

Cameron shook her head. "Nope."

"So it's completely impossible to live up to this standard?"

"Yup."

Allie tossed the magazine onto the coffee table. "It just seems so unfair that women have to strive for an ideal that doesn't even exist in the natural world."

"Welcome to the twenty-first century," said Cameron.

"It's funny how different things were when Eve was a star. Like, you watch her old movies, and sure, she's totally beautiful, but her body looks normal. Her arms aren't really skinny or muscular. She has hips and everything."

"I know, and remember that beach scene where she was wearing that old-fashioned bathing suit? Her ass looked huge," said Cameron. "I guess she was working in the days before StairMaster and liposuction."

"Don't talk about Eve's ass like that."

"I'm sorry. I just think it's fascinating the way notions of beauty change over time."

"I think it's kind of sad," said Allie.

"It's not if you think about it. Look how far science has come. If you're really unhappy with something about your body, or if you have some flaw or whatever, you can always pay to have it fixed. Although at the same time, it does raise the bar for competition. That's my problem. Now being beautiful takes so much money and time and effort."

"If you want to devote your time to that."

Cameron frowned. "You'll never understand, Allie."

"What's that supposed to mean?"

"You never had braces, and you have amazing boobs that you don't even appreciate. You're always hiding them behind a sports bra."

Allie crossed her arms over her chest. "That's because I play sports."

"Still, if I had your chest, I'd flaunt it."

"Well, you will pretty soon, right?"

"That's the plan," said Cameron. "Hey, are you going to the Motion Picture Home tomorrow?"

Allie nodded. "I'm there every afternoon for two more weeks."

"So what's Eve Santora like? Is she still beautiful? She totally seems like the type of woman who could never get old and wrinkly."

"She's still beautiful," Allie said automatically.

"She's got to be ninety, right?"

Allie shrugged. "I don't know."

"You know she used to date Cary Grant."

"Mom told me."

"Do you ever ask her about what it was like?"

"Um, we don't really talk about her past. I think she left LA for a reason."

"Do you think I could meet her? Maybe you can bring me

along sometime so I can take pictures of her for my portfolio?"

"I thought you were done with that," said Allie.

"I thought so, too. But Selby Chasen totally trashed my work, so now I need to start from scratch. So will you ask her for me?"

"Sure." Allie felt weird about bringing Cameron in to gawk at the Motion Picture Home residents. Still, she agreed to ask because she figured Eve would never go for it.

"Thanks." Cameron turned on the TV and flipped through the channels until she got to *TRL*. It was just ending and soon they heard the familiar theme song of *MTV I Want a Famous Face*.

"I love this show," said Cameron.

"I hate it," said Allie. "It's so gory. I can't watch."

"Oh come on. It's so funny. All these people are such losers. Half of them want to be strippers or pose for *Playboy*. I mean, what kind of goal is that?"

Allie shrugged. "Is it so different from what you want?"

Cameron glared at her. "Just because I want to *look* like a *Playboy* centerfold doesn't mean I want to *be* a *Playboy* centerfold, okay?"

"And that's so much better?" asked Allie. "I don't get it."

"Well if you don't get it, I can't really explain it." Cameron turned up the volume. She didn't like this new, self-righteous attitude her sister was sporting. Allie sounded like Blake, the two of them pretending they were above all the vanity. Well, they had that luxury, because neither of them had suffered like Cameron had. Making friends had always been easy for Allie. She wasn't Miss Popularity, but she'd never been tormented like Cameron.

Not that she should need that experience to understand.

Wasn't it obvious that looks mattered? All Allie had to do was look at their mother. If Julie hadn't been born beautiful, she never would have been discovered. Perhaps she'd still be working at the Dairy Queen in the middle of nowhere.

The world was kinder to beautiful people. It gave them more options.

When the commercial ended, Cameron turned back to the television, where the mysterious, faceless announcer said, "For years Krista Sellers has been told she looks like Julie Davenport. Today she wants to make that more of a reality."

Cameron and Allie looked at each other for confirmation.

"Did she just say—?" asked Allie.

Cameron nodded, and both of them screamed when a picture of their mom filled the screen. It was a publicity still from *The Deepest Bluest Sea*.

"I can't believe this is happening. It's so surreal," said Allie.

"I love that picture of Mom," Cameron said. "She looks so beautiful."

The television announcer went on. "Krista will get cheek implants, a nose job, liposuction on her thighs, and a tummy tuck to get that fresh, classic, all-American look that Julie Davenport made popular in the late eighties."

Krista came on camera. She did look like their mom in an eerie sort of way, but she was heavier and her hair was too dark. "Twenty years ago, Julie Davenport was the most beautiful woman in America. People used to tell me that I looked like her all the time. But then I gained fifteen pounds and I can't take it off. I want to move to LA to become an actress. I think that if I look more like Julie Davenport, it'll help me get work."

"Is she for real?" Allie was truly horrified.

Cameron laughed and bounced up and down on the couch. "I can't believe this. This is exactly what I'm talking about, Allie."

"It seems so wrong. Are they allowed to do this without asking Mom? Because she's going to freak."

"Are you kidding?" asked Cameron. "This is totally flattering. Mom will be thrilled."

"She's going to hate this. It's so gross and I don't want some mom clone walking around."

Cameron didn't take her eyes off the television. "Don't worry. They never really turn out like who they want to look like. That's what makes it so tragic."

At the commercial, Allie glanced at her sister. "If I get a nose job, Coach McAdams won't let me try out for varsity soccer next year."

"What do you mean? That's none of her business. She can't do that just because of your nose."

"It's because I'll be missing a week of the soccer camp."

"But you totally deserve to be on varsity. She's discriminating against you for wanting to improve your looks."

"If I don't play, then she's going to pull up Quincy, I just know it."

"Okay, I get why that would be annoying, but in the long run, who cares? It's just a game. You can always quit and do yoga instead."

"I don't know."

"Oh, come on. It's so much fun. Half the class is spent sitting around and gossiping. Sunshine, our instructor, is totally chill. She has this awesome tattoo of a dolphin on her ankle and she tells the coolest stories about when she used to live on an ashram in India."

"I like playing soccer."

"Well, you're going to love your new nose, Allie. Seriously. It'll change your life."

"What if I don't want to change my life?"

Cameron looked at Allie. "I know what this is about."

"You do?" Allie was so hopeful. If Cameron knew what this was about, then maybe she could explain it, because Allie wasn't so sure.

"You're scared, but don't be," Cameron told her. "It's painless. And I know that you've heard horror stories. We all have.

But it's a simple surgery. You're going to be beautiful."

The commercials were over, and both of them turned back to the TV, where they proceeded to watch a silver-haired, overweight doctor in Arizona cut Krista open, suck out the fat, fix her up, and then sew her back together again—in the image of their own mother.

CHAPTER SEVENTEEN

When Cameron caught her first glimpse of Eve Santora, the Hollywood legend who was once described as the most beautiful woman in the world, she found it hard to hide her disappointment. She'd asked, and Allie had told her that Eve was still gorgeous, yet the woman in front of her was wrinkled, thin, and old. Not graceful, elegant old, either—just plain, ordinary old. Even worse, she was printer-paper pale, with eyes so sunken into her skull that one could hardly make out the blue. It was eerie.

"Ms. Santora, it's so nice to meet you. Thank you for agreeing to let me photograph you. It's a huge honor." Once Cameron recovered, she reached down to shake Eve's hand and half-curtsied. She couldn't help it. Despite what the woman looked like, she was still Hollywood royalty.

"Eve, you're sure you don't mind doing this?" Allie asked as she gently rested her hand on the old woman's shoulder.

Cameron had no idea what her sister was so worried about.

Apparently, neither did Eve. "I said I'd do it," she replied gruffly. "So let's get this nonsense over with."

Cameron was taken aback by Eve's rudeness, but only briefly. Allie had warned her that the woman might be cranky. And sure, Eve called the photo shoot nonsense, but she was all dressed up, in black slacks and a fancy red top with billowy chiffon sleeves. She wore makeup, but not too much, like a lot of the residents Cameron had noticed on their walk to Eve's bungalow. She wore just a touch of mauve lipstick and a thin layer of blush—enough to show she was making the effort, to prove that she cared about how she looked. This display of vanity made her more human in Cameron's eyes.

"I could set up in here," said Cameron, walking inside and looking around. "Although the walls are a bit too cluttered. You don't mind if I take down a few of these paintings, do you?"

"Why don't we go outside? There's a nice spot by the Japanese garden," said Eve.

Cameron nodded. "Okay, whatever makes you happy." She would have preferred to work indoors, where she could control the light, but Allie had made her promise to do whatever Eve wanted.

"And don't photograph me in this," said Eve, motioning to the wheelchair.

Cameron readjusted her backpack and put her tripod under one arm. "That's fine. Is there anything else?"

"No, we can go now," said Eve.

As Allie wheeled Eve to the garden, Cameron struggled to keep up. "Thank you again for agreeing to this. I've seen all your movies, and I've been dying to meet you ever since I found out my little sister actually knew you."

Eve didn't even acknowledge Cameron, which was annoying. Was the woman that hard of hearing? Cameron was speaking as loudly as she could without actually yelling. But maybe she had to yell . . .

"What was it like, working with Cary Grant?" Cameron shouted.

Allie shushed her. Whoops. Cameron had promised not to pry into Eve's past, but how could she not ask, when Eve must have so many amazing stories?

Still, the woman didn't answer her question.

Once they made it to the garden, Allie helped Eve out of her chair and onto the bench. It was a lengthy procedure. By the time Eve sat down she seemed winded. Cameron hadn't realized how delicate the woman really was. It was sad.

"How's this?" asked Eve, raising her chin, ever so slightly.

"Perfect." Cameron set up her tripod a few feet away. "I'm going to do a bunch of portraits first. You don't have to pose, or anything. Just act natural."

"'Act natural,'" said Eve. "That's always been one of my favorite oxymorons."

Allie and the old woman shared a laugh, although Cameron hadn't meant to be funny. She fiddled with her tripod, raising and lowering it until her lens was at eye level with Eve.

"Aren't you a bit too close?" asked Eve.

Cameron locked the tripod into place. "I'm going for something dramatic, so the closer I am the better." She wanted to get each and every one of Eve's wrinkles but knew better than to say so.

As Cameron started shooting, Allie looked around. "It's so quiet out here today."

"Everyone is at tai chi on the other side of the lawn," said Eve.

"You guys have tai chi? What a cool place," said Cameron. "You're so lucky."

"You wouldn't say that if you had to live here."

The straight-on shot wasn't very interesting, so Cameron took her camera off the tripod and kneeled down in front of Eve.

"Are you trying to shoot up my nose?"

Hoping that the question was rhetorical, Cameron ignored it.

Taking pictures of her friends had been so much easier. They did whatever Cameron told them to and liked it. Eve looked miserable. "This isn't working," Cameron said. "It's overcast, so I'm going to need the flash."

"That's too bright," Eve said a few moments later, holding up her hand and turning away.

Cameron did her best to stifle a groan. She couldn't win with this woman.

"Are you getting tired?" asked Allie. She turned to Cameron. "Stop it for a minute, okay?"

"Sure, we can take a break." Cameron placed her camera on the ground and searched through her backpack. When she found the pictures she was looking for, she handed them to Eve. "I found these online and printed them for you."

"What are they?" asked Eve, reaching for the shots.

"They're old movie stills from *An Oriental Sunrise*. Don't you recognize yourself?" Cameron leaned over Eve's shoulder and looked. "You were so gorgeous, Eve. I mean, you still are."

Eve's hands shook as she handed them back. "I don't need to see these. I know what I looked like."

"Okay," said Cameron, raising her eyebrows at Allie. For some reason, Allie gave her a dirty look. "Let's get a few more before the light changes again. You're doing great."

"I'd like to lie down," Eve said.

"We'll take you back in a few minutes. I'm almost done here." Cameron lifted her camera. Through the lens she saw that Eve was pensive. Shiny tears appeared in the corners of her eyes. Finally she was getting some real emotion. Cameron shot as fast as she could, but Eve wouldn't sit still.

"Are you all right?" Allie asked, taking a few steps closer.

"Please don't move. This is such a great shot. Allie, can you back up? You're in the frame."

Eve twisted around and placed both of her hands on one arm of the bench. "I'm leaving," she said. "I've had enough of this."

"Wait," Cameron cried.

"Careful." Allie hurried over. "Let me help you."

"I don't need your help." Eve was half standing when she jerked away from Allie and lost her balance. Reaching out to steady herself, her fingertips grazed the arm of the bench. Letting out a surprised, "Oh," she tumbled to the ground.

Allie rushed forward, asking, "Are you okay?"

Eve moaned softly.

"Do you want me to get a nurse?" Cameron crouched down and placed her hand on Eve's shoulder, which felt surprisingly thin and bony. "I'll call for help."

"Please don't," said Eve. "I'm just surprised. Allie, if you could help me up."

Allie put her arm around Eve and helped her stand as Cameron watched helplessly. "I'm so sorry," she said. "I don't know what happened."

"I'm fine." Eve smoothed out the wrinkles in her pants. "Please stop making a fuss."

"What's going on here?" someone shouted from down the hill.

Cameron turned around and saw that a tall, dark-haired woman was rushing toward them. “Who’s that?” she asked.

Allie cringed. “It’s Nancy, the volunteer coordinator.”

When she got closer, Allie tried to explain. “Eve fell off the bench, but she’s okay now.”

Nancy put her arm around Eve, protectively, as if Allie and Cameron would harm her. “No one is allowed to photograph our residents without getting the proper approval, and Allie, you certainly can’t bring strangers here.”

“Um, I’m sorry, Nancy. This is my sister, Cameron. Yesterday I asked Eve if she’d pose for her, and she said yes.”

“There are channels you must go through. Asking Eve isn’t enough. You’re going to have to leave the grounds now.” Nancy pointed toward the exit gates. “Please hurry, or I’ll call security.”

“I’m going,” said Cameron, holding up her hands and backing away. She’d no idea why this woman was so worked up. “I’m really sorry. Allie, I’ll meet you out front at six o’clock, okay?”

Nancy had begun to wheel Eve away, but stopped and turned around. “Allie, you can go now, too.”

“But my shift starts in a half an hour,” Allie said.

“Not today it doesn’t.”

Allie couldn’t believe this was happening. “But I still have another two weeks of volunteer work.”

“I’m not so sure about that. What you’ve done is a blatant violation of our rules. Even worse, it was dangerous and irresponsible. Eve could have been seriously injured."

"I'm fine," Eve said, but Nancy was too upset to hear her.

As Nancy whisked Eve away, Allie called after them. "But I didn't know about the rules. I'm really sorry."

Nancy didn't answer, and soon they disappeared around the corner.

"What's her problem?" asked Cameron as she put her camera way.

"Shut up, Cameron," Allie replied, pushing past her and heading toward the parking lot.

Cameron didn't get it. Obviously Eve was okay. She'd said so herself. So why was Allie so upset?

What was it with everyone these days, making a big deal out of such small things?

CHAPTER EIGHTEEN

"I heard about this one guy who went to Mexico for a nose job because it's cheaper there, and after they took off the bandages, his entire nose collapsed. There was nothing left, and his bone was coming out of the skin. Like Michael Jackson, but worse," Quincy said. She dipped another tortilla chip into the guacamole. "This is so good, Allie. Did you make it?"

"My mom did."

"No respectable surgeon would ever take out that much bone and cartilage," Carly replied.

"I never said the doctor was respectable," said Quincy. "It happened in Mexico."

"Well, you can't compare anyone to Michael Jackson. The guy has had so much surgery his face is more plastic than flesh and bone. His existence gives a bad name to the entire profession."

"Of course you'd say that," said Quincy. "Your dad's a plastic surgeon."

"He's a cosmetic surgeon, not a plastic surgeon. And he's the best." Carly batted her eyes. "I'm living proof."

Allie's friends laughed and she tried to join in, but she couldn't figure out what was so funny. In fact, she had begun to regret inviting them to sleep over in the first place. How could Carly joke about her surgery in front of Allie, who knew there was so much more to the story?

Carly had a Chinese dad and a Norwegian mom. With her shiny dark hair, blue eyes, and narrow nose, Carly looked like both of them. But her almond-shaped, "Asian" eyes had always bothered her. She'd wanted more of a crease, so her dad had double-lidded her eyelids over Christmas vacation.

Before the surgery, Carly had complained that she didn't fit in with her Norwegian cousins or her Chinese ones. Part of it was because she lived in LA and didn't speak Norwegian or Chinese, but she was convinced it had more to do with how she looked. Carly said she felt out of place everywhere, and she hoped the surgery would help with the issue. She'd once cried over it to Allie, so it surprised Allie that Carly could talk about it so casually now, treating the surgery as if it had been nothing more significant than a trip to her hairdresser.

Of course, that was old news. Maybe Allie was taking it all too seriously. She had started to realize that at Bel Air Prep, the nose job after freshman year was practically a rite of passage. It was almost as commonplace as the new car at sixteen and the graduation trip to Europe at eighteen.

Other than Carly, Larkin was Allie's first friend to go under the knife. Her entire family had cancelled their vacation to their Hawaiian time-share so she could fit into Dr. Hsu's schedule. Even for one of his daughter's closest friends, he was that busy.

"You're sure she's coming?" asked Quincy.

"There's no reason she shouldn't," said Carly. "My dad took the splint off yesterday. He said she looks great."

"I talked to her this morning," said Allie. "She's been in bed for three days straight and will do anything to finally get out of her house."

"I just can't wait to see it. I'm gonna freak," said Quincy.

Allie felt a nervous fluttering in her stomach. Quincy's interest in plastic surgery bordered on obsessive. Even now, Quincy was glued to her laptop, looking at awfulplasticsurgery.com, a website devoted to celebrity plastic surgery.

"Check out this picture of Jessica Simpson," said Quincy. "Her lips are all lopsided, like she had a bad reaction to a collagen injection."

"I saw her at the Ivy last month and she's not that pretty in real life," said Carly.

"That's because those pictures in magazines are totally fake," Allie said. "The only reason all those models and actors look so perfect is because of the airbrushing and Photoshop. Sometimes they even use other people's bodies."

No one even looked up from the computer screen. Allie couldn't tell if it was because she was stating the obvious, or because her friends didn't believe her. It was the truth, though. Cameron wouldn't lie, especially not about something as important to her as photography spreads.

"So did Jessica Simpson go to your dad?" asked Quincy.

Carly shot Quincy a dirty look. "Not for her collagen," she said.

"What about Paris Hilton?"

"Look, I don't even know. My dad won't tell me these things. But I heard she has her work done in New York."

"Allie, is your mom freaking out about that MTV thing?" asked Quincy. "It must be so weird for her."

"She's got a good sense of humor about it," said Allie. "I think it bothers me more than it does her. It's just really strange to think about. That woman sold her car and spent her life savings so she could afford to look like my mom. And it's not like my mom is some supersuccessful actress. She hasn't worked in years."

"Those shows give cosmetic surgery a bad name. No self-respecting doctor would allow themselves to be featured on reality television," said Carly.

"I think I hear a car," said Allie, relieved that she could finally change the subject.

All three of them jumped up and ran downstairs.

As Allie opened the front door, she stifled a gasp. Larkin stood on the front step, looking nauseous and unsteady on her feet. Her nose was swollen and red, and her eyes were bloodshot, with purple puffy bags underneath.

"Are you okay?" asked Allie.

"She's fine. She just bruises easily," said Larkin's mom, who stood behind her with two pillows in one hand and a backpack in the other. "Don't touch her face," she ordered. "Her head needs to stay elevated, and she should ice her nose in an hour, and then every two hours until you girls go to bed."

"Mom, I know all this," said Larkin. "You don't have to boss around my friends, too."

"Do you want the swelling to go down, or don't you?" asked Mrs. West as she placed Larkin's stuff inside the door. "And don't make her lift anything heavy above her head."

"What would they possibly make me lift?" asked Larkin.

"This is a bad idea. I should take you home."

"I'll be fine. Please just go."

"We'll be careful," said Carly. "If there's any problem, I'll call my dad."

"Don't forget to ice it," said Larkin's mom.

"Good-bye," Larkin said.

"And be careful," her mom added as she headed back to her car. "That nose cost us a fortune."

Once in the house Larkin rolled her eyes. At least it looked like she rolled her eyes. It was hard to tell because they were so squinty and red. "I get surgery and she thinks that gives her license to be a total bitch."

"Tell me everything." Quincy grabbed Larkin's hand and practically pulled her upstairs. "Did it hurt? Did you hear them breaking the bone? My neighbor Justin said that when they did his nose two years ago, he could hear them sawing."

"There's no way," said Carly. "Unless they used a local anesthetic, and doctors don't like doing that when they operate on teenagers. There aren't even saws involved. If anything, he heard them filing down the bone."

"Ignore her," said Quincy. "She's been acting doctory all night."

Before they made it to the bedroom, Allie's sister walked by.

"Oh my gosh—Larkin, you did it. Let me see!" Cameron exclaimed. She grabbed Larkin by the shoulders and checked out her nose from every angle. "It's gonna look so great, I can already tell. Just wait until the swelling goes down. You'll be gorgeous."

"Thanks," said Larkin.

Cameron looked at Allie. "Madison from Dr. Glass's office called. They—"

"Wait!" Allie yelled.

Cameron blinked. "What?"

"I need to tell you something. In private." Allie widened

her eyes and tried to tell her sister, telepathically, to shut up. Then she turned to her friends, who were still huddled around Larkin. "I'll be right back."

"What's the matter with you?" asked Cameron, once they were in her room.

Allie closed the door behind them and lowered her voice to a fierce whisper. "Are you crazy?"

"What did I do?"

"Please don't talk about my nose job in front of my friends."

"Wait, you haven't told them that you're doing this?" asked Cameron.

Allie shook her head. "It hasn't really come up."

Cameron laughed. "You are such a freak show, Alliekins. You really need to chill. Your friends won't care. Larkin just had one and they're going to find out sooner than you think. Madison called because they have an opening this Monday."

Allie felt a surge of panic well up in her chest. "Monday as in three days from now?"

Cameron nodded.

"I can't do it. I have to be at the Motion Picture Home on Monday."

"You mean you're not fired?"

"I don't think so. Nancy called and said she wanted to see me. She wouldn't make me go all the way down there if she wasn't willing to take me back, right?"

"I guess not. But what about soccer?"

If Allie took the earlier appointment, she wouldn't have to miss a week of camp. And if she didn't miss a week of camp, she'd be able to try out for varsity. She didn't know why she was even hesitating. She only knew that Monday was too soon. She wasn't ready. "I already changed my flight to Colorado, and if I back out of volunteering now, it'll look bad, especially after the other day."

"So you don't want it?"

"I guess not." Allie knew she might be making a huge mistake.

"So you don't mind if I take the appointment instead?" asked Cameron.

"You really want the implants that soon?"

"Of course. I'd do it in a second," said Cameron. "I'm so sick of people telling me not to go through with it, I just want to get it over with."

"Go ahead," said Allie. "You can have it."

"Thanks." Cameron gave her a hug. "You're the best."

As soon as Allie walked through the door, Larkin asked, "What was that about?"

"Um, nothing."

"Who's Dr. Glass?" Carly asked.

Allie thought fast. "My allergist. I need to see him next week."

Luckily, her friends didn't question her any further. They were too busy comparing Larkin's new nose to Keira Knightley's.

Quincy looked up from her computer, briefly, to state the obvious. "Your sister is so beautiful."

Thanks to Dr. Glass, Allie thought but didn't say. Her slight pang of jealousy was soon replaced with guilt and regret. Cameron *was* beautiful. Allie couldn't deny it and she couldn't criticize—not when her own nose job was still scheduled in just a couple of weeks.

CHAPTER NINETEEN

Cameron spent Sunday holed up in her room studying her latest pictures, amazed that the ones of Eve had turned out so well. In person she hadn't seemed all that special, yet somehow her image translated into something powerful on film. Her face was so expressive, and her eyes alive and intense. Even her wrinkles were interesting.

The shots were vibrant, honest, and textured—the sort of thing Selby Chasen might like. Cameron felt like she was on the verge of saying something significant with her work. She just wasn't quite sure what it was. And she didn't have enough fresh material to put together an entirely new portfolio.

When her cell phone rang, she saw that it was Ashlin and rolled her eyes. The rest of her friends totally supported her decision. Even Lucy had come around, apologizing for not defending her earlier, and even admitting that she was jealous. Cameron didn't know why Ashlin insisted on giving her such a hard time. It was too late. She'd be having surgery in less than twenty-four hours. "Hi, what's up?" asked Cameron.

"Listen to this," said Ashlin. "There's a girl in Texas who had saline implants put in when she was nineteen years old and it ruined her life. Right after the surgery she started having shooting pains in her arms, and then over time every single joint in her body starting hurting. Her ribs burned, and her feet ached so much, she could hardly walk. She had trouble swallowing and breathing, and she was dizzy and had tremors. She gained thirty pounds and was eventually diagnosed with rheumatoid arthritis and chronic fatigue syndrome. At nineteen years old."

"Ashlin, you sent me the link to that website this morning. I've already read all about her."

"This is someone else. There are tons of stories like this. As soon as this girl got her implants removed, her health improved, but not completely. She's on disability and can't work a regular job. She will never recover."

"Is that the only reason you're calling?" asked Cameron. "Because if it is, I'm hanging up."

"I just want to make sure you know what you're getting into. Implants only last an average of seven to twelve years. That's according to manufacturers' studies. So you're definitely going to need more surgery, and it gets expensive. You'll have to spend about fifty thousand dollars over the course of your lifetime, and that's if you're lucky and you have only minimal complications. Also, some health insurance companies refuse to cover women who've had implants, and did you read about Olivia Goldsmith?"

"I did, and okay, you were right. She died, but that was a fluke. Her complications started before they even cut her open. Her body just had a weird reaction to the anesthesia."

"Because anesthesia is dangerous."

"I did fine the last time I was under," Cameron reminded her.

"But why take the risk a second time? You're beautiful and smart and you have everything going for you—"

"Good-bye." Cameron slammed down the phone.

She felt like screaming. Staring down at the pile of photos on her bed, she realized that nothing was right and she had no time to fix it. Her family was going to the annual Motion Picture Home benefit party tonight and she had less than two hours to get ready. Cameron gathered all of her pictures and placed the entire pile in her bottom desk drawer before hopping in the shower.

When she was finished, she put on her robe and headed to her closet. She took out the dress hanging in back and carefully laid it on her bed. It was vintage Dior, light gray with black lace and a plunging neckline. Her mom had worn it to the Academy Awards twenty years ago, the year she'd been nominated. Julie claimed she'd been saving it all those years for her daughters, yet when Cameron had asked to wear it to the prom, her mom had said no. The problem was, the dress didn't fit on top, and Julie had refused to let a seamstress near it.

Cameron trailed her fingers along the beaded neckline longingly. Since she couldn't make the dress fit her body, she'd just have to make her body fit the dress.

After putting the gown away, Cameron quickly slipped on the one she had chosen for that night. It was turquoise silk and clingy, with spaghetti straps. Not as spectacular as the vintage one, but still nice, especially with her spiked heels.

As she applied her final coat of lip gloss, her father knocked on her door.

Cameron didn't need another conversation about her "dangerous and shallow" decision to improve her body, but her dad would be driving them to the party, so it wasn't like she could refuse to speak to him. "Come in," she called.

Her father opened the door and stepped inside, leaning against the wall awkwardly. Cameron didn't know what made him more uncomfortable, wearing a tuxedo or being in the same room with her. "You look very nice," he said.

Cameron knew she looked good. She didn't need to hear it from him. "What are you doing here?"

"Calling a truce. This is silly. Please know that it's not too late to change your mind, but if you go ahead with this, I'll still love you, and I'm still very proud of you."

"My surgery is tomorrow, Dad. Of course I'm going

through with it. I wish everyone would just leave me alone."

"I'll be the first," said her dad. "I won't say another word about it. Ever."

"Thank you."

"Mom told me you're upset about the Selby thing."

"Well, yeah. She hated my work."

Her dad wrinkled his brow. "I heard she said you had great technique and an excellent sense of composition."

"I'm sure she felt like she had to say something nice because she's a friend of Mom's. She hated the content. That's what matters, and she's right, too. I need to start over. I've already taken some new pictures, but I'm running out of time. After the . . . well, after tomorrow I'll be out of commission for a while. I wish I could shoot tonight."

"Why don't you?"

"You know they never let people bring cameras to these things. I'm afraid it'll get confiscated. And it's not like it would fit into my purse, anyway." Cameron's evening bag was barely large enough to hold her lipstick.

Her dad walked over to Cameron's camera and took it off the tripod. "I can sneak this in."

"You'd do that?"

"Of course. What else am I wearing this penguin suit for?" He tried to wedge the camera into his cummerbund, but it wouldn't stay in place. Shrugging one arm out of his jacket, he slipped the strap over his shoulder and held the camera to his side. When he put his jacket back on and tried to button it, the two lapels wouldn't meet.

Cameron laughed. "I'm not sure that's going to work."

"I'll figure something out," he said. "Don't worry."

"Thanks, Dad."

"It's my pleasure. Now, let's get going or we'll be late."

Cameron loved, loved, loved black-tie events: school dances, movie premieres, charity galas, Christmas parties, awards shows, anything where people had to look their best, and especially when she got to go with her mom, who always got lots of attention.

Tonight Julie looked stunning in a sparkly silver gown. Even Allie was dressed up in the low-cut navy blue silk dress that Cameron had talked her into buying.

When their car pulled up to the valet stand in front of the host's beautiful Beverly Hills mansion, Cameron gasped. The place was enormous: three stories of pristine red brick held up by imposing Greek columns. Orange and grapefruit trees lined the stone path to the front door, where a crowd of people waited to get past security. News crews and camera-people stood on the lawn, carefully documenting all of the beautiful people attending the party. The paparazzi were never allowed inside, but this didn't stop them from showing up everywhere worth being.

As soon as they got close to the house, the photographers

started yelling. "Julie Davenport, can I take your picture?" "Come say hello to the camera, Julie." "Can we talk to you for a minute, Julie?" "Over here, Julie . . ."

Cameron watched as her mom stopped to wave and beam at the camera. Before she moved on, she put her arms around Cameron and Allie and called out to the throng. "Take a picture of me with my beautiful daughters."

This was Cameron's favorite part. She slipped her arm around her mom's waist and leaned in close, tilting her head and smiling like she'd practiced. Her heart was pounding in her chest, and she hoped her face wasn't too flushed. She tried to keep from squinting in front of the too-bright lights.

"I just wish I could be here in a few weeks," Julie whispered. "After the surgery."

Cameron had been thinking exactly the same thing. If only she had her implants. If only she'd been able to fit into the vintage Dior tonight. Careful not to let her smile falter in front of the cameras, Cameron answered through clenched teeth, "There'll be other parties."

"Thanks so much. Enjoy your evening," someone called. It was a not-so-subtle way of being dismissed.

Before Cameron knew it, the photographers had pointed their cameras elsewhere. Moments like these always went by too fast, but at least she still had the party.

Jumpy, jazzy music trilled from all around. People moved in and out of the many large rooms, air-kissing, sipping drinks, chatting, and laughing. In bland tuxedos and suits, the men faded into the background like shadows. The women always mattered most at these events—all bright and shiny and on display like the rows of jewelry in the windows of Fred Segal.

Cameron marveled at it all: the bright colors, the sparkle, the sequins and diamonds, the silk, the chiffon and lace. The dresses were all different, but underneath them everyone was pretty much the same. Faces were lifted, foreheads Botoxed, lips plumped full with collagen. Ribs were removed as often as cheekbones were added. Thighs and bottoms were liposuctioned to perfection. Noses were turned up cute, and breasts swelled large, alert, and at attention. Everyone striving for perfection.

Cameron got her camera from her dad, who'd had no trouble hiding it in his jacket, and moved through the crowd. She took pictures not of whole women but of body parts: a breast here, an ear there, a piece of cleavage. She zoomed in on noses and eyes, elbows and legs, a daintily sculpted bicep. Perhaps she would construct the perfect woman out of the parts of many. A photo-real Frankenstein.

Eventually, a familiar face appeared in the corner of Cameron's frame. Eve was sitting at a near-empty table. And the only person with her was Allie.

Cameron aimed her camera at them and snapped some pictures. All of the surrounding tables were full, which was sad. It must be hard for Eve, thought Cameron. She was once the woman everyone wanted to talk to, and now she had an audience of one. It was her own fault for leaving this world and letting herself fall apart. She must have realized her mistake, since she had come back for more. Too bad it was much too late.

A tan, handsome man with wavy dark hair walked in front of Cameron's lens. She lowered her camera and called out to him.

Dr. Glass turned around, befuddled. Glancing to the right and then to the left, he approached her carefully. "Can I help you with something?" he asked.

"It's me, Cameron Beekman. You'll be seeing me tomorrow."

"Of course," said Dr. Glass. When he smiled, the skin around his eyes crinkled. It made him look kind of old. Cameron was surprised he hadn't gotten that taken care of. "You look lovely, Cameron, and I'm sorry for my surprise. I know at least half of the women here, but they'd never associate with me in public."

Cameron blinked. "Why not?"

"Think about it. If you're caught talking to me, then it's almost proof that you need me."

"But that's so unfair. This crowd would never look this great without you."

Dr. Glass took a sip of his drink. "It's nice to be appreciated. I'll see you tomorrow." He patted her on the shoulder and walked away.

Suddenly, the lights blinked off and on. Then the MC announced that everyone should quiet down so the ceremony could begin. Cameron went to find her parents' table.

Some of the Motion Picture Home residents were about to be presented with lifetime achievement awards. It was nice of the benefit committee to recognize them, thought Cameron. Not that she planned to sit around and watch. It was eleven thirty and her stomach was growling. She handed her camera back to her dad and slipped away from the table in search of food. Because of tomorrow's surgery she couldn't eat or drink after midnight.

After Cameron found the buffet table, she wolfed down crab cakes and chicken satay and miniature goat cheese and arugula quiches, finishing just in the nick of time. As the clock struck twelve, she took her last sip of water and threw away her cocktail napkin.

It was all so evocative of Cinderella. Better, though, because for Cameron the stroke of midnight marked not the end but the fabulous beginning of her new and improved, more beautiful, brand-new self.

CHAPTER TWENTY

The Motion Picture Home benefit was the last place that Allie wanted to be, but she didn't have any choice. Her dad had gotten the tickets two weeks ago, and at the time she'd been happy that her family was supporting the home. Of course back then, she hadn't realized it would be a black-tie event covered by *Entertainment Tonight* and the E! channel.

"This is a benefit for an old-age home. Why do they need security here?" asked Allie as they waited in line to get into the tacky Beverly Hills mansion with its horrible faux-Greek columns. It was so large and imposing, it reminded her of a hotel. And who would ever want to live in a hotel?

"Tickets were expensive and there are a ton of celebrities here," her dad explained. "There could be crashers."

"Oh." Allie felt silly for missing the obvious yet again. This wasn't just a benefit. It was an *event*, and she should have known. Why else would her mom and sister make her buy a new, fancy dress if not for the cameras?

She stepped forward carefully. The heels made her whole body pitch forward, which turned walking into a huge pain, but Cameron had insisted that she wear them. Apparently, they were the only pair that went with the outfit, which Allie couldn't stand either. Whenever she showed too much cleavage, guys talked to her chest rather than to her face. It was creepy.

"Julie Davenport, can I take your picture?" someone yelled once they got close to the camera crews.

"Of course," Julie replied.

This was Allie's least favorite part about going to events with her family, which said a lot, because there was so much not to like.

Her mom pasted on a smile and turned toward the camera. Julie excelled at that type of thing. It was so easy for her to turn into someone she wasn't. When Allie was younger, it scared her.

Before she moved on, Julie stopped and put her arms around Cameron and Allie. "Take a picture of me with my daughters," Julie said, and she and Cameron struck matching smiles, as if they'd practiced. Allie tried it as well, but she sensed she'd gotten it wrong. Maybe they'd cut her out of the final shot. More likely, none of them would make it in in the first place. Her mom wasn't exactly a big star. Allie felt bad about that and then wondered why she even cared. Not being featured in some dumb magazine wasn't exactly a tragedy.

Julie whispered something to Cameron, but Allie couldn't hear what she was saying. Maybe they were complaining that it was all taking too long. It seemed as if they were standing there forever. The bright lights hurt her eyes. She glanced at her dad, who stayed well away from the cameras. How come he was allowed to avoid such nonsense?

Once inside, Allie's parents stopped to talk to some friends, and her sister went to take some pictures—of what, Allie didn't know. Abandoned, Allie felt panicky at first, but then relieved because she wouldn't have to pretend like she was having a good time.

Conversations competed with the band, making it all too loud. Beautiful people mingled everywhere, air-kissing and fake-laughing and checking each other out. Even though Allie's dress was smooth and silky, she felt like she was trapped in an itchy wool sweater.

She walked through room after room in search of some peace, but instead she ended up in the dining area and found Eve sitting at a table by herself.

A bunch of photographers crowded around the cast of some new ABC drama. Eve sat watching it all with a strange smile on her face. Allie cut through the crowd and sat down next to her.

"Hi, Eve. How are you?" she asked, as she slipped off her shoes and wiggled her toes.

Eve's face brightened. "Well this is a nice surprise," she said.

"I feel horrible about what happened the other day. I never should have brought my sister there in the first place. I'm so sorry."

"I'm fine. Please don't worry."

"I didn't know I was breaking any rules. Honestly."

"You were just trying to do a nice thing. It's a silly rule. They're afraid we'll be exploited, but really they should worry more about us being ignored. That's much more damaging, in the long run."

"My sister wasn't trying to exploit you."

Eve patted her hand. "I told Nancy that it wasn't your fault, and that she needed to hear your side of it."

"We have a meeting tomorrow," said Allie.

Eve nodded. "I know. She'll let you come back. I've made sure of that. But I still don't understand why you'd want to."

"I have to," said Allie. "I mean, well, you know I have that requirement."

"There are other ways you can fulfill it, I'm sure, besides spending time with a bunch of old people."

"What if I like old people?" asked Allie.

"Well, then there's something wrong with you. Look around." Eve gestured toward the other tables, which were all full. "It's as if they're worried that old age is contagious, and maybe they're right. You should be careful."

Allie laughed, asking, "Where are the other residents?"

"Oh, they're backstage getting ready for some lifetime recognition awards." Eve lowered her voice and gave a convincing imitation of a radio announcer. "You're still alive. Congratulations. Yes, we ignore you most of the time, but your existence has given us a wonderful excuse to throw this fabulous party."

"Aren't you supposed to be with them?"

"You're not going to turn me in, are you?"

"I wouldn't dare." Allie looked around. "God, I hate being at things like this."

"I used to love them."

"Do you ever miss it?" asked Allie.

The cool thing was, she didn't need to specify. Eve understood.

"Of course I miss it. The problem came when I needed it, and when it meant everything to me. Those pictures your sister showed me? I was upset because my arms looked too fat. That was the first thing that struck me. Then I started worrying about my eyes because my left one was squinting closed. Sixty-seven years it's been since that was taken, and I'm still worried about how I looked."

"You were beautiful," said Allie.

"Yes, I was, wasn't I? And thank you for using the past

tense. I hate it when people lie and tell me I'm beautiful now. I am a wrinkled and lumpy old woman in an unflattering dress, but that is all I can be at my age."

"I'm sorry." Allie said it without thinking, but what was she apologizing for? The shallowness of the world? The fact that everyone got old?

Eve shook her head. "Don't be. It's not important. There are other things to care about. If you spend so much time worrying about how pictures will turn out, what you look like, and what others say and think, well, that sort of thing can drive a person crazy. And the thing is, there's no end to it. No one ever thinks that they're beautiful enough. There's always more you can do."

"Is that why you left Hollywood?" asked Allie.

"Let me tell you a secret." Eve leaned forward and lowered her voice to a whisper. "I didn't leave Hollywood. Hollywood left me."

"But everyone said you chose to leave."

"I had some wonderful public-relations people," said Eve. "At the time I still cared about what the world thought. I knew that my career was over, and I needed my disappearance to be dramatic."

"That doesn't make any sense. How could your career have been over when you'd won all those awards and you were loved by millions?"

"People loved my image. If they'd known the real me . . .

well, let me just say that things were different back then. I had to hide some things about my personal life because the public wouldn't have understood. In the end, it was too great a sacrifice. Some things are simply more important than fame. I have no regrets about what I left behind, because I've had a very full life."

"What have you been doing all this time?"

"I spent my life with the woman I loved. We traveled a lot, and eventually we moved to Europe. That's when I took up painting."

"Those pictures in your apartment, then . . . you painted them?"

Eve nodded, slightly. "Yes, most of them."

Allie was amazed. "Why didn't you ever say anything?"

"What would have been the point?" asked Eve. "I did them for myself, not for outside recognition."

"But you could have told me."

"There you are," said Julie, walking over to their table and sitting down next to Allie. She reached across and touched Eve's wrist. "You look so beautiful, Eve. That's a lovely dress."

Allie cringed, afraid that Eve would disagree and that her mom wouldn't understand. Her mom, who cared too much what everyone thought. Her mom, who tried so hard to please.

But Eve just smiled and winked at Allie. "Thank you, dear," she said. "So do you."

CHAPTER TWENTY-ONE

Cameron woke up feeling woozy and confused. As she blinked, her surroundings came into focus, but not completely. She felt like she was wearing someone else's glasses. Everything in the room was blurry, with no defined edges. She tried to sit up but couldn't. Regardless of how hard she willed her limbs to move, they hardly stirred. At least she managed to emit a low moan.

Moments later the patient coordinator—someone familiar and beautiful—walked over and placed a gentle hand on Cameron's shoulder.

"Mahh." Cameron felt relieved that she wasn't alone but also embarrassed because she couldn't seem to make any other sound. She'd meant to say "Madison," but it had sounded like something between a moo and a call for her mom.

"We're all done here, Cameron. Congratulations. You did great."

Cameron tried to sit up.

"Don't worry about moving until you're ready. Stay here for as long as you'd like."

Cameron was ready, or at least she wanted to be. She tried to say as much, but her tongue was too thick and swollen and her throat too dry. She felt like she had something large and heavy on her chest—not just a boulder, more like a small mountain range.

"Why don't you go back to sleep?" Madison suggested.

This sounded like a fine idea, so Cameron closed her eyes and drifted off.

When she woke up the next time she was able to form actual words. "Hello?" she asked.

Madison turned to her and smiled. "Are you thirsty?"

Cameron nodded, so Madison brought her some ice chips, helping Cameron raise her head before tilting back the small plastic cup, ever so gently.

"Trust me, the first few days are the hardest," said Madison. "But you'll get through it. Does it hurt?"

Cameron swallowed. Her chest felt stiff and constricted like the day after a superintense workout. The pressure was dull but definitely present. "A little," she managed to croak out.

Madison said, "I'll go get your mom."

A minute later Julie rushed into the room with Allie trailing close behind. Cameron was so happy to see them, she felt like crying.

One of the nurses helped her into a wheelchair and brought

her out to the car, which her mom had driven around to the exit at the back of the building. Then, with one arm around Madison and one around the other nurse, Cameron was helped into the backseat. What should have been a simple task took an enormous amount of effort. Cameron had never felt so helpless and it scared her. Too weak to put on her seat belt, she stretched out across the backseat and closed her eyes.

The next thing Cameron knew, she was at home and in her own bed. She didn't remember how she'd gotten there, but at the moment she didn't care. Sleep felt glorious. She spent the day in a fog, in sheer exhaustion.

Cameron's mom and sister moved in and out of her room, bringing her ginger ale and crackers, dry toast, some lukewarm tea. She felt plenty of pressure and dizziness, but the actual pain didn't start until early the next morning.

Moaning, Cameron looked around. She saw a bottle of Vicodin on her bedside, a glass of water next to it. She gulped down one pill and closed her eyes.

The pill turned the pain into something fuzzy. It made her float. Yet it made her wired as well as groggy, so she was only able to sleep fitfully. Because it would have hurt too much to sleep on her chest, she stayed on her back. She was sick of looking at the ceiling and found it impossible to get comfortable. She wanted to scream in frustration, yet she felt too weak to raise her voice.

When Cameron woke up next, her mom was sitting in a

chair next to her bed. She had no idea of the time. The sun filtered in through her lowered blinds. That meant morning, perhaps afternoon.

"How do they look?" She had to ask, because her breasts were encased in a gigantic surgical bra. It was twice the size of a normal sports bra, and more like a corset, really.

"It's too soon to tell, honey." Julie smoothed down Cameron's hair. "But don't worry. I'm sure they'll be beautiful. We're going to see the doctor tomorrow."

Cameron looked down at her swollen chest, but the effort it took exhausted her. She drifted in and out of sleep, and before she knew it, her mom was waking her and helping her dress for her appointment.

In the examining room, Dr. Glass removed the surgical bra. "Let's see what we've got," he said.

Her bare flesh felt cold. She glanced at her mom, whose face remained blank, and then at Madison, who grinned and winked.

Dr. Glass examined the incisions under her nipples.

"I'm going to show you the mirror, but before I do, I have to warn you. You're going to hate me when you see yourself. Right now your breasts are extremely swollen and riding too high. They'll look and feel stiff, too, but I promise you, the swelling will subside and they'll come down and get softer."

When Cameron caught her image in the mirror, she had to struggle to keep from crying. She felt like a train wreck and looked even worse. Her too-pale face and greasy hair were nothing compared to her chest. Her boobs were enormous. Larger than Pamela Anderson's, which she wouldn't have thought was possible. The stitches looked scary and the incisions on the undersides of her nipples were inflamed. Also, her breasts were pointy—like large, swollen torpedoes.

"They'll look better next week. Okay, Cameron?" Dr. Glass re-covered her chest with the surgical bra.

Too upset to speak, she just nodded and turned away from the mirror.

"You'll probably notice the changes every month or so. It'll take an entire year to see the final results, but by the time you leave for college in the fall, they'll look great."

Cameron remained silent. It was hard to imagine that her chest would ever look great.

As Dr. Glass headed for the door, he said, "Madison will walk you through the massaging exercises. You'll do them along the edges of the implants, twice a day for a month. This should help minimize the risk of capsular contracture. I'm also writing you a prescription for some scar-reducing cream. You'll need to rub it into your wounds for the next six weeks to help with the healing process."

Before he made it out of the examining room, Julie spoke up.

"She told me that the pain is really bad, and she's not sleeping well."

"That's completely normal," Dr. Glass assured them.

"But isn't there anything else you can do?" asked Julie.

"All she needs is time to heal," Dr. Glass promised. He smiled at Julie. "I'll see you next week."

When she got home, Cameron crawled back into bed and tried to console herself by looking at the digital-imaging shot of her chest taken weeks before. She ran her fingertips along the picture, longing for the day when her breasts would look that perfect.

At the office it had seemed so easy. By pressing a few keys on his keyboard, Dr. Glass had transformed her. Cameron had fooled herself into believing the surgery would be that simple, as well. Sure, she'd been told about the complicated and painful recovery process. She'd spent hours doing research on the risks and arguing with her dad and with Ashlin, but deep down she hadn't really thought about what it would feel like. It seemed so obvious that her body would need to adjust. Incisions had been made under each of her nipples, and two silicone envelopes had been pushed through and placed underneath her chest wall muscle. Then 350 cc's of saline solution had been pumped into each one. Of course it would hurt. She had just happened to overlook that because she was so focused on the fun part: throwing away her padded bras and replacing them with cute, lacy lingerie; buying new bathing suits and going to her first college party in a tight tank top.

Now there was no way not to think about the pain all the

time. Her ribs ached, and she couldn't feel her nipples. Her entire right breast was numb, while her left breast hurt like crazy. Her stitches were starting to itch, too. The Steri-Strips that covered them had turned yellow from the pus. She'd asked Dr. Glass to remove them, but he assured her that they'd fall off themselves in just a few days' time. Cameron didn't want to wait.

She needed it all to be over, because things that should have been easy were now so complicated. Cameron wanted more than anything else to shower but would not be able to for three more days. She dreaded going to the bathroom, because it hurt too much to stand up and walk by herself. Whenever she did manage to go, all she could do was pee, because the Vicodin made her constipated. Her stomach felt cramped and bloated.

Crawling back into bed, she took another pill for the pain and cried until she was too tired to cry any longer.

When she woke up, the house was quiet and dark. Cameron couldn't sleep anymore. She'd been sleeping for too long.

Easing herself out of bed, she went over to the mirror, took off her shirt and bra and stared. Her boobs were still swollen. Being a patient required so much patience, Cameron thought. Was that why the words were so similar?

When she got tired of looking at herself, she glanced around her room. Her portfolio sat on her desk, underneath a pile of magazines. She hadn't looked at it since her nightmarish critique. Flipping through the pictures of her friends posing on the beach, she could kind of see Selby's point. They really weren't about anything except pretty faces and great bodies. The shots were interesting to Cameron because they represented her success after so many years of lonely struggle, but that was personal. She hadn't managed to convey that with her photos, which meant her pictures weren't about anything larger. They weren't thought-provoking, and they didn't say anything to the outside world. Regardless of the pain, she needed to do something about it.

But what else did she have? Cameron took out the box of her recent prints and started going through them. The pictures of Eve had turned out great, as had the ones at the benefit, but Cameron didn't know how she'd pull it all together. She needed more pictures to work with, and since she was confined to her bedroom, her options were limited.

Her new camera rested on its tripod in the corner. Cameron moved it to the center of her room and aimed the camera at her unmade bed. Taking off the lens cap, she peered through. Then she set the self-timer and walked around to the other side. Sitting down at the foot of her bed, she stared into the lens blankly as the camera flashed and clicked.

Self-portrait of a girl who wanted to be more beautiful. On the digital display screen, her eyes were open, and she looked as if she were posing for a mug shot. Topless.

Cameron lay down on her back and held the camera above, pointing down.

She took close-ups of her bare breasts—both together and then one at a time—from various angles. The shots were gruesome, but they were also realistic and gritty. She liked them.

Shooting her swollen, stitched-up breasts reminded her of Orlan, a French performance artist she'd studied in art class. Orlan had been having and documenting serious plastic surgery since 1990, using her own flesh as a medium to communicate and to inspire debate.

There were many stages to Orlan's work. First she provided surgeons with computer-generated images of facial features that have been idealized as feminine beauty in art. Then she actually had the surgeries. She'd given herself Mona Lisa's forehead, the nose of Gerome's Psyche, and the chin of Botticelli's Venus. Later on, in an attempt to mimic Mona Lisa's protruding brow, she'd had implants—the kind normally used to enhance cheekbones—placed above her eyebrows. The results were grossly exaggerated. In the end, it looked as if she were growing small horns.

Her public exhibitions included not just pictures and videos of her surgeries, but actual vials of her blood and fat that were left over from them. Disgusting but powerful. Her goal was to suggest that beauty as an objective was unattainable and that the process was horrifying.

Cameron got what Orlan was saying. It was annoying that women had to try so hard. But Orlan was not the eighteen-year-old daughter of a former model/actress; nor was she on her way to the University of Santa Barbies. Understanding the horror and futility of achieving perfection didn't mean that Cameron was somehow immune to striving for it.

She continued taking pictures, hoping it would all translate into something she could use.

Two days later, Cameron could sit up and go to the bathroom without pain. She was off the Vicodin, so her whole stomach issue was resolved. Her ribs ached, but that was manageable with aspirin. Cameron was up and walking around without a problem. The Steri-Strips had fallen off and her incisions still itched like crazy, but she'd switched from the uncomfortable surgical bra to a regular sports bra. That helped, although she still had to wear it at all times—even in her sleep—because it hurt not to.

Her friends called, wanting to see her. First Lucy came and brought balloons. Then Hadley and Taylor showed up with flowers. Even Ashlin visited, leaving behind a very sweet card that read SO CAN I HAVE YOUR OLD WONDERBRAS NOW?

Everyone thought she looked great, and they were all very supportive, but the one person that Cameron really wanted to talk to never even called.

She thought about Blake a lot and went through the pictures of him that she'd accumulated over the past year: Blake strumming his guitar; Blake doing a handstand on the beach, his ugly beret lying next to him in the sand; Blake wearing a tux on the night of their homecoming dance. The last shot made her angry, but she wasn't sure why.

Where was he now? After all they'd been through, it seemed impossible that their relationship was over. How could it be when everything felt so unfinished?

CHAPTER TWENTY-TWO

As Allie staggered into the kitchen, red-faced and out of breath, her mom hardly looked up from the stove. "You went running again?" she asked.

"I was just practicing wind sprints," Allie huffed. She still hoped that if she was fast enough, she could prove to Coach McAdams that she deserved a shot at the tryouts even if she missed a week of camp. "What are you doing?"

"Cameron was craving pudding."

Allie glanced at the staircase worriedly. "I didn't realize it would hurt so much."

"It won't be so bad with your nose."

"Where's Dad?"

"Working."

Allie's dad never worked on Saturdays. Of course, he never worked past eight o'clock either, but he'd managed to miss dinner with the family every night that week. Clearly he was avoiding the house because of Cameron. Even though they'd talked and things were supposedly okay between them.

Allie poured herself a glass of water and sat down at the kitchen table. Although she didn't say anything, her mother seemed to read her mind. "Don't worry. Your father will come around. He was so dead set against this. It'll just take him a while."

"It's not like you wanted her to do it either," said Allie.

"Of course not, but I understand where she's coming from. And your sister is very stubborn. She knows what she wants and who am I to judge? I knew what I wanted when I was eighteen."

"Did you ever wonder what your life would have been like if you hadn't been"—Allie was about to say "beautiful" but stopped herself—"discovered?"

"Of course," said Julie. "I'd be stuck in Wisconsin and it would have been miserable because I never would have met your father and I never would have had you girls. Things were different for me. I've told you that. College wasn't an option. I didn't have the grades or the money."

"So why do you think it's so important to her? I thought she was happy. She seems happy, you know?"

Julie finished making the pudding and joined Allie at the kitchen table. "Cameron is so ambitious, it scares me sometimes. She's so driven. I feel like she'll do anything to get her way. Part of me admires her for knowing what she wants and for going after it. Your father has the same drive, and that's part of why he's so successful. But it's worrisome, too. I wish Cameron would focus her energies on obtaining something more tangible. Beauty is complicated, slippery. If she doesn't know that yet, then she's going to learn it someday. Yet at the same time, I understand what she's after. And why shouldn't she want to be as beautiful as she can be?"

"What if she becomes addicted to this? Like, what if this is just the beginning?"

"I don't think that'll happen."

"Are you nervous about your face-lift?"

Julie reached for Allie's hand and squeezed it. "A little," she said. "Are you nervous about your procedure?"

Frowning down at the table, Allie didn't answer right away. "I guess. It's weird to think about, you know. It seems like the whole thing is out of control. Did you watch that MTV show we TiVo'd for you?"

"I did, and it was creepy, but that's an extreme, Allie. There's a big difference between having one procedure to improve your own looks and reconstructing your entire self in the image of someone else."

"I know, but don't they sort of both come from the same impulse? Do you ever feel like maybe you just shouldn't give in?"

Her mom seemed to consider the issue carefully before answering. "It's not giving in, Allie. At least, that's not how I see it. You're too young to understand, but try to imagine that you once had this amazing power to make anything happen. At first you were awed by it, and then you loved it, and then you got used to it and assumed it would always be there. Then all of a sudden, long after you'd taken it for granted, it was gone."

"But it wasn't just gone. You left the business because you wanted to."

"I'm not just talking about my career. And yes, I took time off when I had you girls, but do you know why we moved to LA?"

"Because Dad got a new job here."

"Dad got a new job here because I asked him to. I wanted to start working again, and I needed to be here. I've been auditioning for three years, Allie. And it hasn't led to anything."

"You could have told me."

"I didn't want to. Children shouldn't have to worry about their parents like that. I made my choices and I don't have any regrets. In the end, I'm glad I've been there for you girls. That's certainly more important. I just wish I could have done both."

"You always said that Hollywood was so superficial, that you hated being judged."

"Knowing that it's a ridiculous game only makes it harder. I don't know why it's so important to me, but it is. Especially now. You girls have your own lives. You don't need me like you used to. It's time for me to go back to work, and this is all I know."

"You know what Eve told me the other night? She said she didn't even leave Hollywood by choice. Not completely. She said that Hollywood left her."

Her mom smiled at her, like she didn't believe her.

"It's sweet of you to try and make me feel better," Julie said as she stood up. "I'm going to check on Cameron now. Do you want to come?"

"That's okay." Allie watched as her mom left the room.

Eve had given up her fame and career for something more important. Beauty hadn't been enough. Allie wanted to tell her mother, but she didn't know how. Perhaps it wouldn't have done any good anyway. Everyone knew that looks didn't last forever. Maybe it was okay to stretch things out for as long as possible.

CHAPTER TWENTY-THREE

It wasn't just in mirrors, but in windowpanes and other shiny surfaces too—the stove top and the coffeemaker. Every time Cameron caught a glimpse of herself, she was stunned, but in a good way.

It had been almost two weeks since her surgery, and her breasts finally looked like actual breasts. They were still too large, but not obscenely so. Strangely, they seemed fragile, like precious foreign objects that were too beautiful to touch. When Cameron showered, she was afraid to let the water hit her chest directly. Driving made her nervous. She was afraid she'd crash and they'd deflate. But that was all psychological, and Cameron tried not to obsess over it, because she had more important things to do.

All her recent pictures were spread out across the floor of her room. She sifted through them in search of a unifying theme.

Before the photo shoot in Cabo, Cameron's friends had spent hours—all morning—getting ready for a shoot that had lasted less than half as long. Cameron had managed to get it all on film: Lucy applying her first coat of lipstick, Taylor curling her eyelashes, Ashlin brushing out her hair, Hadley dabbing cover-up on her chin. Now she realized that these candids were actually more interesting than the pictures her friends had posed for. They all looked more beautiful when they weren't trying so hard.

Cameron added the pictures to her portfolio and moved on to the next group.

The portraits of Eve would definitely be included.

As would many of the Motion Picture Home benefit ones. Strangely enough, the most interesting picture from that night had been taken accidentally. Cameron had meant to capture a group of photographers taking pictures of a beautiful new actress. In the background of her shot, though, was Eve, sitting alone at the table, watching. The picture evoked real feeling. One looked at it and yearned to know what the frail old woman with the intense gaze was thinking.

This was unexpected. Cameron had always loved that pictures could lie. Now she saw that they could also reveal the truth.

Her obsession with body parts, for instance. The numerous breast and cleavage shots from the party made a striking contrast to the images of Cameron's postsurgical chest. Her inflamed red stitches and her swollen and pointy torpedo breasts were gruesome but necessary. Like the process of beautification.

It came to her in a flash. Her work was about youth and beauty and age and beauty and celebrity and beauty and the work people do for beauty, and the futility of it all as well, because everyone will someday look like Eve. Old, wrinkled, frail, and close to death. Regardless of how many plastic surgeries you can afford. The process of aging, nature itself, cannot be conquered.

Everything happened seamlessly from that moment. Cameron knew exactly where to place each picture. It worked out perfectly, as if she'd envisioned it that way all along. She was so excited about the final result, her hands trembled as she turned the pages of her book. This was something good, something real that she'd created.

"Hello, Cam?"

Cameron looked up, surprised. She'd been so wrapped up in her work, she hadn't even noticed her sister in the doorway. "Hey, Allie."

"Blake is here. Should I tell him to come up?"

"What? No! It's a mess in here. I'm a mess." She ran her fingers through her bangs, annoyed that she still cared. Jumping off her bed, she said, "Tell him I'll be down in a minute."

Cameron threw on a baggy sweatshirt, then looked at herself in the mirror. Why was she hiding her chest from Blake?

She didn't know, but there wasn't time to contemplate. There were other, more pressing questions. What did he want? To remind her of how shallow she was, yet again? To tell her it was all a horrible mistake? Or to admire her chest?

She didn't want to see him and she was dying to see him. She missed him terribly and she was angry with him for not calling or visiting sooner. Elective surgery was still surgery, and Cameron had really suffered—regardless of her motivations. Even Ashlin had been great about coming to visit. Her criticism had stopped the day Cameron had her breast augmentation.

Grabbing her portfolio, she headed downstairs. Blake stood in the foyer, looking sheepish with his hands in the pockets of his baggy shorts.

"What are you doing here?" she asked, and then regretted sounding so cold. Then again, Blake looked at her chest before he looked at her face. That hurt.

"Hi, Cameron. How are you feeling?"

At least he was now focused on her face. Not that she was ready to forgive him. He was so deliberate about making eye contact, she could tell it took effort, that he really wanted to check out her chest. "I'm okay now. Nice of you to wait so long to make sure, though. Thanks for that."

"I called your house the night after your surgery."

"How did you know?" asked Cameron.

"You mean because you changed the date? I ran into Allie

at Griffith Park a couple of weeks ago. I asked her not to tell you. I just wanted to make sure you were okay, and I guess I figured it would upset you too much to talk to me."

"Upset me or upset you?"

"Both of us, I guess." He shrugged, looking down at his feet. "I should've come sooner, but I felt weird about the whole thing. I'm sorry."

Cameron felt her eyes tear up. As much as she missed Blake, as much as she wanted to forgive him, she couldn't. She was still so angry, and it wouldn't be fair to make it this easy for him. Sure, now that the worst was all over, he'd probably be glad her boobs looked so great. Or would once the scars faded. It seemed silly, but she didn't want to give him the opportunity to enjoy them.

"You should have thought of that before you called me shallow," Cameron said.

"I think we both said a lot of things that we regret."

This was true, but she wasn't going to admit it because that would mean agreeing with him. "Come look at my portfolio," she said instead. She grabbed his hand and pulled him farther into the house. "I just finished and I'm sending it off tomorrow."

They sat down at the kitchen table and Cameron watched Blake flip through the images—smiling at her friends' goofiness and cringing when he made it to the shots of her breasts postsurgery. It was uncomfortable showing it to him, but worth it because he reacted to every page. Sure, some of his reactions were of disgust, but that was okay. Cameron wasn't ashamed of what she'd done.

"These are amazing, Cam. I don't know what to say. You did it, though. I'm sure you'll impress that photographer."

Cameron wished she didn't care what Blake thought.

He closed her portfolio. "I'm sorry I didn't come sooner and I'm sorry if I was a jerk in Joshua Tree. It's just . . . I don't get you. You're so talented and driven, and this portfolio is awesome. How can you be the same person who cares so much about her looks?"

"Everyone cares about what they look like. You're not above it, Blake. I'm sure you'd like to think you are, but you're not. You took a shower this morning, and you brushed your hair and picked out those clothes. Yes, your shirt has a hole in the sleeve, but you're making an aesthetic choice by wearing it. By actively not caring about your image, you're choosing to present yourself to the world in a very specific way."

"Oh, come on, Cameron. You know what I mean. It's the extreme stuff that I don't get. Hair and makeup, fine, but this is different. Someone as smart as you shouldn't feel like she has to surgically alter her body in order to conform to society's artificial standards of beauty."

It was frustrating that he still didn't get it. "I didn't feel like I had to. I felt like I wanted to. And I'm not going to apologize for being a complex person. I'm allowed to appreciate art and be ambitious and still want to be beautiful. You can't pretend that what I look like doesn't matter."

Cameron felt Blake's legs bounce under the table. "I've been thinking about what you told me out in Joshua Tree, how everything changed after your nose job, and it all makes sense to me now. I get your insecurities, and it's okay. No one is perfect, you know? We all have our flaws, and I forgive you."

Cameron narrowed her eyes at Blake. She saw him like she'd never seen him before. Clueless. How come she'd never noticed it? "You forgive me?"

Blake reached across the table for her hand, but she pulled away before he could touch her.

"I don't need for you to forgive me. I'm not apologizing."

"Okay, whatever," said Blake. "Maybe that came out wrong. It's just, summer is almost over and we shouldn't waste any more time."

Suddenly something occurred to Cameron. "Remember the homecoming dance last fall?"

"Sure." Blake shrugged. "We'd just started going out back then."

"Right. And I was elected homecoming queen, and I wanted to pose for portraits after, but you refused."

"It's such a cliché, posing for pictures at a high school dance. Who needs that?"

"I do," said Cameron.

"Well, the homecoming court is stupid. All those ceremonies do is glorify monarchies. It's so elitist. Feudal, even."

"It was democracy," said Cameron. "They voted for me."

"Okay, I'm sorry." Blake threw up his hands. "Look, all I want is for things to be good again. So you're right. We should have posed for pictures that night. Do you still have the tiara? Because we can do it right now."

"It's too late." Cameron spoke sharply, surprising even herself. "I want to break up."

Blake smiled, as if he thought she was joking. "Wait, what? You're breaking up with me because of homecoming? That was, like, ten months ago."

"It's not just that. It's because you think there's something wrong with me for caring about stuff like that. You think I'm shallow, but the thing is, Blake, you weren't the only person to object to my surgery. Everyone else, though? They did so because they were worried about my health and all the risks involved in breast augmentation. All you've talked about is my image, and that makes you just as guilty as me."

Cameron stood up and headed for the door. "You should have come to see me sooner. Calling my sister to check up on me wasn't enough."

Blake shook his head, dazed, as he followed her to the entryway. "So this is it?"

"We're just too different."

He was halfway to his car when it occurred to Cameron

that she wanted to hug him good-bye—to tell him that she didn't have a lot of regrets, and that things had been really good for a while. Perhaps it was better that she didn't, because the faster he was gone, the harder it was for her to change her mind.

CHAPTER TWENTY-FOUR

Groggy and still half-asleep, Allie sat in the passenger seat of Cameron's car. It was eight o'clock in the morning. Surgery day. Her sister had basically recovered and was running a sort of shuttle service that morning, dropping Allie off for her rhinoplasty at the front of the surgi-center, then going around back to pick up their mother after her face-lift.

"Aren't you excited?" asked Cameron, glancing at Allie. "You don't seem excited."

"I'm excited." She said this because it was easier to agree.

Turning back to the road, Cameron frowned. "You must be nervous."

Allie shrugged. In truth she was terrified. At the thought of being put to sleep, of being cut open, of having to face her friends afterward, and of turning into someone who cared more about clothes and hair and makeup than about soccer.

Sure, she loved Cameron, but that didn't mean she wanted to *be* Cameron.

"You're acting like you're on your way to a funeral."

"It's not something I can get too excited about, you know? It's just my nose. Just something I have to get through."

Cameron pulled up to Dr. Glass's building. "Do you want me to go up there with you?"

"No, don't worry about it."

Before Allie managed to open the door all the way, Cameron reached over and gave her a hug. "Good luck. And just so you know, it's not too late. You don't *have* to get a nose job if you don't want one."

Allie pulled away. "Of course I do. Mom and Dad signed me up. This is important to them."

"But it's your nose," said Cameron.

"Obviously."

"No, I'm being serious. It's okay to be nervous, but just make sure this is what you want. No one is forcing you to do this, you know?"

"I'll be okay," said Allie, getting out of the car and heading into the building.

Once she made it upstairs, she was surprised to find that Dr. Glass's office was nearly deserted. Madison sat at her desk overlooking the empty waiting room. "Good morning, Allie. Good news. I just saw your mom, and she's out of surgery. It went really well."

Allie felt so relieved. "Can I see her?" she asked.

"Oh, there isn't time. We're going to be ready for you in just a couple of minutes. Why don't you have a seat until then?"

"Okay." As Allie sat down, she glanced at the stack of magazines on the coffee table nearby: *Vogue*, *Cosmo*, *Vanity Fair*, and *Marie Claire*.

An actress on one of the covers was in the latest blockbuster, and according to Cameron she was Dr. Glass's patient. Allie picked it up and studied her image. Her skin was smooth and her breasts were large. She was deeply tanned and her legs were long and slender. She was beautiful. Impossibly perfect. What would it be like to be that stunning? Allie couldn't believe she was thinking of things in those terms, now, especially now that she knew looking like that was impossible. Whatever Cameron had must be contagious.

She flipped through the pages of the magazine. There were articles about getting perfect abs, sculpting your triceps, applying eyeliner, and the pros and cons of using lip gloss instead of lipstick. Everyone telling women what they needed. Allie didn't even wear makeup yet, but she was already sick of listening.

The next page she flipped to had a survey: MEN CONFESS: WHICH LOOK GETS YOU ASKED OUT? There were three columns with two women in each one. It was a compare-and-contrast thing, and the survey results were printed at the bottom of the page.

The first column showed a woman in a long black dress standing next to a woman in a zebra-print miniskirt. Eighty-five percent of the men preferred the long black dress.

The article included a quote from Leon, an accountant from Seattle. “The woman in black looks more elegant.”

Yet Jeffrey, a lawyer from New York City, claimed, “I’d go for the tarty animal print. It’s way more sexy.”

The next column featured the all-important long hair versus short hair debate. The results were 73 percent to 27 percent in favor of long hair. Thomas, a painter from Chicago, liked short hair because it was cuter, while Jason, an architect from Kansas City, preferred long hair, which he deemed more feminine. These men weren’t experts or professional stylists. They were just random guys on the street.

“Who cares what they think?” Allie asked, amazed and then embarrassed because she’d said it out loud. The waiting room was empty, though. As happy as she was that no one had heard her talking to herself, she was a little disappointed, too, because there was no one to show this craziness to.

As Allie closed the magazine, Madison walked into the room asking, “Did you say something?”

“No.”

“Are you ready?” she asked.

Allie looked up blankly. The question struck her as odd,

but at first she wasn't sure why. Then she realized that this was the first time anyone had actually asked her. And even though she knew Madison's question was rhetorical, she had to wonder.

Was she ready? Ready for what? To accept some narrow definition of what was beautiful? To strive for an ideal that didn't exist in the natural world? To want the kind of nose that Gary from Minneapolis preferred?

Was she ready to miss a week of fun in Colorado? To sacrifice her spot on varsity? To give it up to Quincy because Quincy happened to be born prettier? And prettier according to whom?

"Last-minute jitters?" Madison smiled down at Allie as if she understood. "Don't worry. It happens to everyone."

"No." As Allie stood up, the magazine slid to the floor, but she didn't bother picking it up. She was too intent on making it to the exit.

"I don't understand," Madison called. "Where are you going?"

Allie didn't answer. She ran out of the office and sprinted down the stairs—five flights—and then out the door onto the sidewalk, where she promptly collided with some guy in a suit.

"Hey, watch it," he yelled, clearly annoyed.

Startled, Allie looked at him. She started to apologize but stopped. How could he be so hostile when he had no idea what she was running from?

He looked at her, disgusted, as if she were insane. It was absurd. Where did he get off?

She laughed a loud, crazy laugh. "You watch it," she told him, and then turned and sprinted down the sidewalk.

At first she just wanted to get as far as possible from the surgi-center, but as she ran she began to recognize her surroundings. It became clear that she wasn't all that far from home.

For so long Allie had struggled with whether or not plastic surgery would make her more beautiful, without ever asking herself why she needed to be. If she needed to be.

Everyone talked about fixing Allie's nose, when it wasn't even broken. In truth, Allie wasn't all that worried about what she looked like to the world. She didn't want to be, because she was much more interested in what she would do in the world.

She ran as fast as she could. Her heart was pounding in her chest, but she didn't feel winded. In fact, she was home before she knew it. It had taken her some time, but she'd finally found her perfect stride.

ABOUT THE AUTHOR

Leslie Margolis grew up in Los Angeles and now lives in Brooklyn, New York. This is her first novel. Before writing *Fix*, she studied social anthropology at the London School of Economics. Her focus at that time was the Latin American peasantry, which somehow led to her current field of study, the elusive North American teenager.

For more information about Leslie and to see pictures of Aunt Blanche, her six-toed genius dog, visit www.lesliemargolis.com.